Antoine Laurain is the award-winning author of novels including *The Red Notebook* and *The President's Hat*. His books are translated into 25 languages and have sold more than 250,000 copies in English. He lives in Paris.

Louise Rogers Lalaurie is a writer and translator from the French. She is based in France and the UK.

Praise for *An Astronomer in Love*:

Longlisted for the Dublin Literary Award 2024

Shortlisted for the Edward Stanford
Viking Award for Fiction 2024

Winner of the Prix de l'Union interallié and
the Grand Prix Jules-Verne 2023

'Perfect for the poolside or sitting outside a café with
a pastis and olives – and bound to give you just the
same cheering lift' *The Times*

'A brilliant love story . . . The supporting cast, including a
not-quite-dead dodo and a zebra, will have readers laughing
and crying in equal measure' *The Lady*

'Cinematic and enchanting' *Foreword Reviews* (starred)

'Simply beautiful. An enchanting dual-timeline story of a
love written in the stars' Fiona Valpy, author of
The Dressmaker's Gift

'A witty, lovely, surprising triumph' William
Ryan, author of *A House of Ghosts*

Praise for *Red Is My Heart*:

'Both enchanting and disturbing. A heartbroken lover's
obsession with his ex is reflected in both images and words'
Washington Post

'This inspired combination of romantic musings and playful
drawings is a collaboration between two great Parisians'
Daily Mail

'The emotional journey of a broken heart laid bare by an exceptional writer' Jenny O'Brien, author of *Buried Lies*

Praise for *The Readers' Room*:

'The plot blends mystery with comedy to great effect, and, as ever, Laurain has fun at the expense of his countrymen' *Daily Mail*

'[An] elegantly written little gem . . . the whole thing is such fun' *Big Issue*

'A stylish whodunnit blended with an affectionate send-up of the world of books' *Sunday Mirror*

'Laurain has spun a fantastically intricate web here . . . Joyously far-fetched and metafictional' *The Herald*

'A brief blackly comic masterpiece . . . An observation on life's rich tapestry; absurd, witty, truthful and engaging' *Crime Time*

Praise for *Vintage 1954*:

'A glorious time-slip caper . . . Just wonderful' *Daily Mail*

'Delightfully nostalgic escapism set in a gorgeously conjured Paris of 1954' *Sunday Mirror*

'Like fine wine, Laurain's novels get better with each one he writes . . . a charming and warm-hearted read' Phaedra Patrick, author of *The Curious Charms of Arthur Pepper*

Praise for *Smoking Kills*:

'Funny, superbly over-the-top . . . not a page too much' *The Times*

'Formidable – and essential packing for any French summer holiday' *Daily Mail*

'A brisk black comedy . . . Laurain's considered tale retains an elegant detachment' *The Observer*

Praise for *The Portrait*:

'A delightful literary soufflé that fans of his other charming books will savor' *Library Journal*

Praise for *French Rhapsody*:

'Beautifully written, superbly plotted and with a brilliant twist at the end' *Daily Mail*

'The novel has Laurain's signature charm, but with the added edge of greater engagement with contemporary France' *Sunday Times*

Praise for *The Red Notebook*:

'A clever, funny novel . . . a masterpiece of Parisian perfection' HM The Queen

'In equal parts an offbeat romance, detective story and a clarion call for metropolitans to look after their neighbours . . . Reading *The Red Notebook* is a little like finding a gem among the bric-a-brac in a local brocante' *The Telegraph*

'Resist this novel if you can; it's the very quintessence of French romance' *The Times*

'Soaked in Parisian atmosphere, this lovely, clever, funny novel will have you rushing to the Eurostar post-haste . . . A gem' *Daily Mail*

Praise for *The President's Hat*:

'A hymn to la vie Parisienne . . . enjoy it for its fabulistic narrative, and the way it teeters pleasantly on the edge of Gallic whimsy' *The Guardian*

'A fable of romance and redemption' *The Telegraph*

'Part eccentric romance, part detective story . . . this book makes perfect holiday reading' *The Lady*

'Flawless . . . a funny, clever, feel-good social satire with the page-turning quality of a great detective novel'
Rosie Goldsmith

FRENCH WINDOWS

ALSO BY ANTOINE LAURAIN:

The President's Hat
The Red Notebook
French Rhapsody
The Portrait
Smoking Kills
Vintage 1954
The Readers' Room
Red Is My Heart (with Le Sonneur)
An Astronomer in Love

FRENCH WINDOWS

ANTOINE LAURAIN

Translated by **Louise Rogers Lalaurie**

Gallic Books
London

A Gallic Book

First published in France as *Dangereusement douce*
by Flammarion, 2023
© Flammarion, Paris, 2023

English translation copyright © Louise Rogers Lalaurie, 2024

First published in Great Britain in 2024 by
Gallic Books, Hamilton House, Mabledon Place, London, WC1H 9BD

This book is copyright under the Berne Convention

No reproduction without permission
All rights reserved

A CIP record for this book is available from the British Library

ISBN 9781913547752

Typeset in Garamond by Gallic Books

Printed in the UK by CPI (CRO 4YY)

2 4 6 8 10 9 7 5 3 1

To P., for ever and ever

Who would we be if we could not sympathize with those who are not us or ours? Who would we be if we could not forget ourselves, at least some of the time? Who would we be if we could not learn? Forgive? Become something other than we are?

Susan Sontag
Literature as Freedom, acceptance speech for the Friedenspreis (Peace Prize), Frankfurt Book Fair, 2003

In the middle of the unevenly cobbled courtyard stands a tall tree. No one has ever quite determined its species; some people in the building see a wild cherry, others an oak, though it has never produced an acorn. To stand beneath its branches, you must enter the courtyard from the south, through the round arch used by horse-drawn carriages long ago. Staircases rise all around – one is of cream-coloured stone, supporting the delicate twists of its wrought-iron railing, but the rest are wooden. Those serving the east wing are permanently dark. The building as a whole – the hallway, staircases and ceilings – is in need of renovation, but no one here seems in any hurry to live with the smell of fresh plaster and paint, let alone to put up scaffolding.

Shadows can be seen passing behind the windows that look down from all sides. One window closes, another is set slightly ajar, filtering sounds from the world within: a song, the TV news, the spatter of a shower, the ring of a mobile phone.

The carriage door closes heavily at your back, and you stand for a few seconds in the gloom, feeling for the once-illuminated switch whose tiny bulb has long since fizzled out. Yellow light spills over the stonework and cobbles from the dusty, opalescent glass lantern. You make for the tree and take out your keys, which jingle faintly as you walk up to your floor by the stone or wooden staircase.

You're inside, you're home. You pour yourself a drink and, as if by instinct, you cross to the window.

She sits herself on the couch and then, very slowly and carefully, she lies down. She must be about thirty. Her pale complexion contrasts with the ink-black hair that falls around her shoulders. I think her eyes are blue. I've never been very good at determining the colour of people's eyes. Just recently, my wife pointed out that my best friend has dark blue eyes, which is quite unusual. I've known him for thirty-three years. If anyone had asked me the colour of his eyes I would have answered: Brown?

Physical details such as this escape me. I see the whole person, nothing else. For Nathalia Guitry, I'd say: a young woman of about thirty, attractive, dark hair, pale eyes. That's all.

Neither of us has spoken for about a minute. I always wait for the patient to break the silence, but in this instance nothing happens. Time passes. You can let the entire hour allotted for the session slip by without anyone saying a word: there's no rule that says the silence must be broken. On the contrary, it can be seen as an introduction, an overture. Silence is not a void.

Nathalia Guitry has never been here before. Indeed, it

seems this is her first-ever therapy session. I could ask her how she found my address, but that has never seemed to me to be of the slightest importance. The patient would very likely give me the name of their doctor, or a friend who comes to see me or has come in the past. But to my mind, this conjuring of other individuals dilutes that initial moment of contact. There should be two people here in the room, the patient and me. No one else. Two is enough. Quite enough.

It is winter. Outside, a fine sleet is falling. As usual, I have drawn the red curtains. The weather has an impact on people with depression; sun, snow, rain, wind, cold, heat, all affect their state of mind in the moment. Here, everything is neutral. Neutrality is essential. My consulting room is conceived as a sort of anti-space, geographically speaking. The patient must forget about their city, their country, their smartphone, their Facebook and their Instagram. The office – I prefer to call it the 'office', it implies the notion of work, which I hold dear – is an Everywhere. An island adrift from one continent to the next, from neurosis to psychosis, melancholy to suffering, dreams to fantasies. The office is a lightship, transmitting its signal. No one is ever caught in its beam by chance. They have sought that guiding light, sometimes without knowing it. And I am the captain of that ship.

'Doctor Faber…?'

'I'm listening,' I say, from the trough between two fifty-metre waves. Sometimes the line of communication crackles with interference: silence, anxiety, fear, slips of the tongue. It doesn't matter. The office remains afloat through bad weather of every kind. Unsinkable, and silent.

'I feel as if I'm in a submarine, you know? One of those immense submarines that runs silently under the thickest ice, in utter secrecy.' A patient told me that once, and I smiled. I should have picked up on the idea of secrecy, of the ice as a symptom of oppression, but in the moment, I was charmed by the seductive image of black metal gliding unseen through icy waters, and all I said in reply was:

'Yes, it's a little like that.' He was happy with this. Reassured. Which was the main thing.

She hasn't said anything further about herself, or the weather, or the person who directed her to me, so I shall break the silence. We'll see.

'Your family name is Guitry. Are you any relation to Sacha Guitry?'

She smiles. One point to me. A slightly bitter smile, but a smile all the same.

'None whatsoever… And anyway, Sacha Guitry never had children.'

Silence again. It must not be allowed to take hold. I'd like to go further with Sacha Guitry; she seems to know her subject. Of course, Guitry may not be her real name – I never check my patients' identities. It doesn't matter who they are. I keep to the basic principles of traditional psychoanalysis – payment for each session in cash, for example. No cheques, no cards, no clues to the individual's identity. I'm a qualified medical doctor, and as such, I must have filled out any number of forms that my patients have never sent off for their treatment to be reimbursed. I keep to the basics of traditional psychoanalytical practice, too: Freudian slips or 'misperformances', for example. I use them sparingly but they're there, like an old set of tools at the bottom of the cupboard. They can prove useful. Sometimes very useful.

'What can I do for you, Nathalia?'

'I think my I've screwed up my life.'

A phrase I hear often within these walls. There are several variations: 'I've screwed up my life' is a definitive statement, presaging a long, often very long, stint of hard work. 'I think I've screwed up my life' hints at the element of doubt. Things are not quite so serious. The patient's life is screwed up, but not explicitly the patient themselves. The life is a thing apart. Like a pet one has had since childhood, but which has always proved unsatisfactory. You live with a fox-terrier, but you realise that what you truly desire is a Bengal cat.

In the case of Nathalia Guitry – who showed no reaction when I addressed her informally, by her first name – what interests me is her use of the word 'think'.

'And what makes you think that?'

'I feel as if I'm not fully alive. My professional life is a failure.'

'And what is it you do?'

She hesitates for just a few too many seconds before answering.

'I'm a photographer.' She smiles apologetically.

'Why do you smile?'

'I'm a photographer who doesn't take photographs.'

'Tell me about that.'

Now, at this precise moment, we are in analysis. That

harmless-sounding phrase marks the first real contact with the patient.

Tell me about that. We're going to talk about them, about their problem, or what they believe is their problem. Unless it proves to be a trap, concealing deeper, far more damaging fault lines.

'I've run out of work,' she tells me.

'And why do you think that is?'

'I've lost my talent.'

Her words have a romantic, disenchanted quality that is not lost on me. But she speaks in a firm, assertive tone that puts me on my guard, more than is usual.

I ask the straightforward, unavoidable question:

'You've lost your love of photography?'

'Yes.'

'And why is that?'

'When you can no longer do the job you love, you lose interest, and you don't love it any more.'

I turn the phrase over in my mind, searching for the fault line, but she goes on:

'It's like with actors. If an actor can't act, they die.'

Fault line. Response:

'Those are someone else's words.'

'You're right. I was photographing a famous actor a few years ago. It's what he told me.'

'So you were getting paid work, before.'

'Yes.'

'And now you're experiencing a lull, and you can't bear it.'

She says nothing. I was expecting another 'Yes.' Nathalia

seems to like answering in the affirmative, which suggests a determined character, perhaps excessively so, but very much alive. So many patients – men and women alike – lie on my couch, moaning endlessly: 'I don't know…', 'Perhaps…', 'Yeahhhh…', 'Hmmmm…', 'Pfffft.' Seconds pass, during which I try to categorise Nathalia's case, however vaguely. For now, I'll put her with the Melancholic Depressives.

'Can you remember the last photograph you took?'

'Yes.'

'What was it of?'

'A murder.'

Nathalia has left. I brought the session to a close just after those last words. Never play the patient at their own game. Life in here is not like life out there. Out there, anyone to whom you announce such a thing will be dumbfounded, shocked. They'll fire questions at you, be transfixed, experience an adrenaline rush. Not here. Here, things are different. She got up from the couch and paid me. We exchanged our mobile numbers. I always do this. The patient can contact me in an emergency, and I can contact them. It's a connecting thread, and we can use it – or not.

I fill out a new client card:

First name: Nathalia

Family name: Guitry

Reason for starting therapy: Has photographed a murder.

Symptoms: Inertia.

Pathology: Melancholic depression.

In another column, I always jot down some initial ideas, anything that occurs to me after the first session. This time, I scribble the words: imagination, truth, mythomania.

We haven't fixed another appointment. It is up to her to contact me again if she wishes.

She lies down slowly and carefully, just as she did the first time.

I want very much to return to the subject of her last photograph, but I sense that Nathalia requires a different angle of approach. Murder, though... Most of my clients come to vent about neuroses of a more everyday kind: problems at work, a complicated divorce, an inferiority complex. They feel disorientated, lost in the modern world – the Covid crisis, international tensions – and they feel its effects in their day-to-day lives, on their savings. Stress. Stress made worse by children who've sprouted suddenly into turbulent teenagers, when they were malleable and charming just a year or two before. Not to mention that perennial classic, the Oedipus complex.

I have two of those: Lemont and Robotti. I really should organise a group therapy session, a weekend in the country, so that the two of them can get to know one another. Together, they might almost be classed as a two-man 'twin complex', to borrow a term from my American colleagues. Two individuals whose neuroses derive from identical causes, and who express them to their analyst in identical terms. Lemont and Robotti

24

were both stifled in childhood by mothers who dressed them in girls' clothes, in secret, until they were six years old. Now in his prime, Robotti tells me that these days he would be considered transgender. Lemont has a subtle variation on the same theme: perhaps he should identify as non-binary? And I sit, and listen, and try to help them acknowledge their feelings. It's difficult, even exhausting at times. It's quite unusual for an attractive young woman to sit herself down on the couch and just talk to me about her creative block. Murder, rather. Not her creative block: murder.

'You've spoken about your professional life, but not your private life.' It's a question I hesitate to ask, but it's a necessary question all the same. Some patients develop an urgent case of verbal diarrhoea when they hear these words. But not here, not now. All she says in reply is:
    'Yes.'
    'Do you want to talk about it?' I ask. But her answer is a reassuring silence. I'm not sure I'm in the best frame of mind for a string of childhood stories, each more sordid than the last. In truth, analysis is quite boring. Every now and then a patient will stand out from the crowd – gifted, intelligent, succinct in their answers – you can spot them straight away.
    Some analysts call such patients their 'assistant', because they assist you in the work of analysis, rather than lying on the couch, passive and unresponsive, waiting for a miracle to descend.
    Questions followed by long silences only really occur in here. Out there, if you ask someone a question and they

don't reply, it introduces what Freud terms 'the uncanny' – a troubling sense of alienation. Here, nothing is uncanny or strange. Everything is normal. And so I wait.

'I don't seem to be capable of living.'

'What do you mean by that?'

'I look at other people's lives and I ask myself: How do they do it?'

'And how do they do it?'

'I don't know.'

'Do you see your camera as a barrier between you and the world, a form of protection?'

'It's a little like that.'

'You aren't taking pictures any more, so the barrier has gone, and you feel vulnerable.'

'Perhaps.'

'What do you do all day?'

'Nothing.'

I wait for her to say something else. Experience has shown that the word 'nothing', firmly pronounced, usually prefaces a whole catalogue of activities. One patient, Guichard, assured me that his Wednesday afternoons were filled with *nothing*, followed by an exhaustive, detailed list of every possible and imaginable sado-masochistic practice, the clubs specialising in said practices, secret addresses and women's first names passed from hand to hand, invariably preceded by the dominatrix's classification number. For Guichard, 'nothing' meant bondage and a whipping from Mistress Caroline in a smartly appointed studio flat in the 6th arrondissement. Not for one second did he think that this particular definition of 'nothing' might be of relevance to our work together. The most perverted individuals are often the most naïve.

'I sleep, and I wish I could sleep for ever.'
  'Do you have suicidal thoughts?'
  'No.'
  'Are you sure?'
  'Yes, I don't want to kill myself.'
  Often, my patients lie. But she's telling me the truth – or I'd like to think she is. If I heard, tomorrow, that she had killed herself with an overdose of barbiturates, I would be genuinely surprised.
  'What else, apart from sleep?' I ask.
  'I write in my diary.'
  'Do you like writing?'
  'Yes.'
  'And apart from writing?'
  'I go for walks.'
  'Where do you walk?'
  'In my apartment... I watch the people opposite. In the north wing.'
  'You watch your neighbours?'
  'Yes. Force of professional habit. I feel as if I'm an eye.'

She has internalised a form of perversion: voyeurism, rendered harmless through the practice of her profession. But Nathalia cannot be a perverted voyeur because she is a photographer by trade. For her, the act of seeing is a continuation of her work.

True voyeurs are never professionally involved with image-making. They are genuine, passionate amateurs, bankrupting themselves with expensive telephoto lenses, infrared and night vision binoculars. They hide in their cars, playing 'I spy', in the Bois de Boulogne or other open spaces. Sometimes, they will visit saunas or naturist beaches, and leave all their pseudo-military paraphernalia in the boot of their car. They are gentle, sensitive, shy creatures, albeit capable of capturing the most sordid scenes on their retinas. They're easily identified: they cannot be touched. They recoil from physical contact like an oyster from a drizzle of lemon juice. I know this. I never shake their hand. They are grateful for that.

'An eye that looks but sees nothing?'
  'Yes.'
  'How many floors are there?'
  'Five.'
  'And what do you see on those five floors?'
  'Stories. Lives. Life.'

Detached from life, but not from the act of looking. Nathalia hides behind her own eyes. Huddled behind the crystal of her lenses like an animal curled in a ball, hibernating in her lacrimal fluid. A foetus in its sac, going back to her first beginnings. She is proving to be a more difficult subject than I had imagined at first. Melancholic depression due to a loss of a professional framework is quite common. It happens with artists, of which she is one, and with executives suffering the consequences of a corporate restructuring beyond their control. As a rule, I try to help melancholics rediscover their interest in life by finding them an activity, however trivial. It's always a step in the right direction. I might ask an executive who's been made redundant to give me their analysis of the financial markets. I'm careful to situate the small task I ask of them – but which may require a superhuman effort on their part – in their particular field of competence. With Nathalia, this is something of a challenge: she doesn't take photographs any more and she hardly ever goes out.

'Nathalia, I'd like to ask you to do something for me.'

'Yes.'

'I'd like to suggest an activity.'

'I don't want to take photographs,' she says straight away.

'That's not what I was thinking.'

The silence settles around us once again. All I can see is her glossy black hair and her delicate hands resting on her skirt. We'll get nowhere like this. Talking has its limits. 'One must find a way to deviate,' said Malevinsky – my mentor and master. Deviation from the spoken word means finding an alternative confessional form. The written word. 'The written word is thought, it *has been thought*, and thought may be expressed in the mouth or from the nib of a fountain pen. It has existence; our body – the mouth, or the hand guiding a pen – serves merely as a vector for that *other, invisible body of thought*, and it is this that concerns us.' Malevinsky again. We write in solitude and in silence, and Nathalia seems quite accustomed to both states. I try an approach:

'You say you watch the occupants of the five floors of

the north wing of your building. I'm going to make a suggestion: a change of strategy for our sessions. We're going to communicate differently, you and I. Here's what I suggest: you will bring a short, written piece each time, about life on one floor of the building. A true story, or one you've made up, it doesn't matter which. And we'll go from floor to floor, starting at the ground floor, then the first, second, third… Up to the fifth floor. Do you think you can do that?'

'And at the fifth floor, we stop?'

'By the fifth floor, we'll have made a great deal of progress,' I tell her.

'You think I'm going to tell you about myself, through these stories?'

She has understood the exercise perfectly, but she seems on her guard. It's my job to bring down those last defences, the sentinels of clear consciousness who believe they are protecting the Self when, in reality, they are stifling it.

'I should like to try this exercise with you.'

'OK, but there's one thing: I won't bring the story with me each time, I'll post it to you. I couldn't bear to watch you read what I've written.'

'Fine by me.'

She pays me, and I remind her that she can smoke during our sessions.

'How do you know I smoke?' she replies.

'I can smell it on your clothes,' I say, with a knowing smile.

Nathalia fixes me with her blue eyes. A questioning look, or a reproach? I cannot tell. All I know is that she sees me. It's a rare thing for my patients to see me quite so clearly. Often, quite deliberately, they avoid my gaze.

The first envelope arrived this morning, 16 January, but dropped into our letterbox by hand, not posted. Brown paper, no stamp, a computer-printed label bearing my name. It surprised me that Nathalia hadn't addressed it by hand, I should have liked to see her writing. Heavy pressure? Sensual? Hesitant? Energetic? Are her Ms and Ns cursive or pointed? Is the letter i merely dotted, or topped with tiny, round planets?

I shall never know. Eleven pages on the subject of 'the ground floor'. Word-processed and stapled together. My wife was very curious about the envelope and eager to read its contents. I was forced to explain that this wasn't some crime novel, but therapeutic work. She was disappointed and claimed she'd been joking. She said I had no sense of humour; I used to be much funnier before.

Before? My patients use that word, too. They wield it all the time, like a talisman: I wasn't like this Before, everything was fine Before, if you'd known me Before. When was this enchanted Before, and when did it end? Is there ever a time in our lives when everything is simple, straightforward, carefree? No, of course there isn't. The past is always reinvented in a better light. We sift our memories to remove the impurities, and the scant specks that remain seem brighter than they were in reality. For my part, I don't really take my wife's meaning. Was I a witty raconteur, Before, full of entertaining stories about my patients, shared over aperitifs, nursing a glass of port?

I don't remember ever having been that man.

Now, I'm settled in my armchair, and I pop my half-moon reading glasses on my nose, the ones I've been forced to wear for a few years now, and lose constantly. Nathalia is due in an hour's time. I'll devote half an hour to reading the sheaf of papers. Perhaps I'll make a few marginal notes. I take out my gold Cross pen, presented to me by the New York City analysts' association, and grandly inscribed: *To J. Faber from the Analysts' Guild of NYC.*

I should say that this is the first time I've asked a patient for a piece of work of this kind. Until now, I've asked them to write down their dreams, or their family memories. 'My grandmother was a wonderful woman...' or 'Last night, I was walking down the street, stark naked.' That sort of thing.

This is different:

My name is Alice Larjac, your personal coach, and I'm here to help you make sense of male/female relationships...

GROUND FLOOR

My name is Alice Larjac, your personal coach, and I'm here to help you make sense of male/female relationships. Welcome to my new video. I always start my videos with these words, spoken with a smile, in a lively tone of voice. I film myself with a camera that can take pictures or shoot footage. A Leica. I set up a few professional lights, check my make-up, part my long, dark hair and bring it around to the front of my shoulders. I always use the same background: I sit on my sofa, with my big, blue Jacques Monory lithograph on the wall behind me, and then I speak straight to camera. My short introduction – quite ordinary, really – is a kind of mantra. I'm up to 278,000 followers on my YouTube channel. That means 278,000 people have signed up, subscribed. As if the whole of Bordeaux and Montpellier had registered to receive my content.

I love what I do. I help people – men and women alike. In just over fifteen minutes, my videos talk about anything and everything to do with love and relationships, with titles like:

She Doesn't Know What She Wants: What Can I Do?

Five Things Women Look for in a Man
Six Signs She's Jealous
How to Spot a Narcissist... and Leave Them!
Love and Manipulation: Is Your Partner Overstepping the Boundaries?
Jealousy: The Spice of Love, or a Passion-Killer?
Five Types of Men to Avoid
Five Types of Women to Avoid
The Florence Nightingale Effect: How to Stop Needing Mr Needy
The Cinderella Complex: You Don't Have to Take Her to the Ball
Bipolar Men in Black and White: We're Going on a Badger Hunt!
Finding the One: Is There Any Such Thing as True Love?

'... are you being a gentleman, or being taken for a ride? It's a fine line. Guys, whenever you feel unsure, *watch yourself.* Don't let her take you for a ride. Know how to say no, and watch how your partner reacts. A well-formulated, tactful, polite refusal should always be accepted. Or perhaps she gets tense, sulky, refuses to talk? Perhaps the atmosphere is suddenly electric? Perhaps there's a heavy silence? Are you walking on eggshells? Do you feel guilty for refusing her something she wants? Above all, remember one thing: toxic behaviour like this will take its toll... on you. A truly loving partner does not sulk – check my video on women who sulk! Just click the link in the bottom right of your screen. That's all for now! I'm Alice Larjac and this has been *Gentleman or*

Poodle? Five Ways to Slip Your Leash. See you next time. Stay well!'

I lean forward and stop the Leica. Another video all sewn up. It'll go online in a couple of days, with a couple of photos: David Niven in his sixties smoking jacket, Martini in hand, and then a black-eyed poodle peering into the lens beneath a great big fluffy pom-pom of fur. The two pictures will flash up quickly, one after the other, when I say the words 'Gentleman' and 'Poodle'. I'm quite pleased with it, actually. The perfect punchline.

I do in-person talks, too. I hire seminar spaces in Paris, Strasbourg, Lyon, Nantes… About eighty or a hundred people each time. I record them, and people can pay to download the recordings from my website. And I accept a handful of private clients for paid telephone consultations. They tell me about their relationship problems, and I tell them what I think. No advice, just my opinion on the facts. Mostly, people are so bound up in their situation that they can't see it for what it is any more. They can't get a handle on it at all. They feel lost, and so they call me. I make money. I have a close circle of regular clients – mostly men, but there are a few women, too.

I'm thirty-four years old. I've been doing this for six years. It started with a book that Aïcha gave me one day. Aïcha's my best friend. The book was called *Perfect Harmony: Understand Yourself and Make Sense of the World*. I frowned when I saw it.

'Another crappy self-help book? Meuf, don't tell me you read this nonsense?'

We hardly ever call one another by our real names. We call each other 'meuf'. It's back slang for 'femme' - woman.

'Listen, I found it in the bookshop. I was going to buy the new Houellebecq... This little book has sold fucking thousands. I wanted to see for myself what it's all about, and you know what? It's not so dumb...'

I rolled my eyes, but I promised her I'd read it. A few days later, I texted: 'I read your thing. You're right. There's some good stuff.'

She texted back: 'Meuf, you could do it a million times better.'

Aïcha and I have known one another since we were eighteen and students, still living with our parents in Paris. I would smoke in secret every evening after class, before heading for home. Always on my own. Just a quiet moment, sitting at a café table. Always the same one. Afterwards, I'd chew peppermint gum to get rid of the smell of cigarettes. And one day, a dark-haired girl came over and asked if I had a light. She went and sat at another table, took a drag on her cigarette, then turned to look at me and smiled:

'Let me guess – a quick cig before going home to Mum and Dad? Chewing gum on the way back...'

I laughed.

'Yep. Exactly that!'

And Aïcha came and sat at my table. I liked her straight away, with her big smile, her doe eyes and her frizzy hair.

'I'm Aïcha,' she said.

'Marie-Edwige,' I told her in reply.

★

Yes, there's something I need to tell you: I'm not called Alice. Certainly not Larjac either. My name's Marie-Edwige de La Tourrière. Nothing destined me to become a YouTube influencer. Or perhaps something did. I wanted to act. I wanted to perform on stage, on film. It was the thing I loved. When I was a child, I adored dressing up, being someone else for a few hours – a princess, or a prince, or a beggar, or a trapper deep in the woods. Anything at all, it didn't matter. I would steal my brother's costumes, and make my own, and get so bound up in the role I was playing that I'd forget who I really was. When someone called me by my ghastly real name, to come and get my snack, I wouldn't understand at first. No one summons a queen or a black-caped bandit to come and have a glass of juice and a piece of cake. At thirteen years old, I announced to my mother that I wanted to be an actor. She slapped me. My father intervened and told me all about this unimaginably dangerous profession, full of ne'er-do-wells, druggies, prostitutes, freemasons and Jews. I went to my room and gazed at the big portrait of Greta Garbo I had hung in a frame on my wall. And the other one of the great French actor Louis Jouvet. I said to myself: this could get complicated.

I'm a perfect specimen of French noblesse, particle and all. *De* La Tourrière, *if you please*. A pure-blood aristo – neither rich nor broke, at ease with a pre-determined set of values and beliefs. I grew up in Paris, in the 7th arrondissement, with all the other Charles-Édouards and Marie-Bérangères whose parents would come to meet them from school, the fathers in pink trousers and tasselled loafers, the mothers with their Hermès bags and their hair pulled back in a ponytail – sometimes even a velvet headband too. I often wondered if there'd been a mix-up on the maternity ward: perhaps I was really the daughter of a famous film director or a top model, handed to my parents by a cruel twist of fate. I've always detested my ludicrous first name, the cross I bore all through my childhood and my teenage years – my father's grandmother's name, and so, of course, it came down to me. The day I told my mother that I believed I'd been swapped on the maternity ward, I got another slap. My perfect brother, Édouard, is the family's pride and joy. He's in the army. He did Saint-Cyr, the officer training school. There's a photo of him in his dress uniform, with his sword, in my father's office. There isn't one of me. Well, there is. Just the one. I'm six years old, in a woolly hat, on a skiing holiday. My parents are way over on the far right, and sometimes they even admit to being royalists. In public, they say they're 'conservative'.

But let's go back to Aïcha. Aïcha comes from the high-rises on the outskirts of the city, and she always knew she wouldn't stay there. In our second year of law school she was top of the class; I was coasting – I never studied.

'We can teach each other so much,' she told me one day. 'I'll tell you everything I know about guys, and girls, and sex, and life. And you can tell me everything you know: your education, your people, how to behave, all that bourgeois noblesse shit. It's a win–win, meuf!'

One day, when we were still students, I took Aïcha home. My father was there with his accountant, and he came to greet us with my mother, who was having tea with a friend of hers. Aïcha said hello to everyone, very politely, and we went up to my room. When Aïcha left, my father opened my bedroom door and stood there, staring at me in silence.

'Your friend is… is North African?' he said, speaking very slowly, in a toneless voice, as if he was announcing the imminent arrival of an asteroid that would blast us all back to the age of the dinosaurs.

'Yes. Aïcha. She's my best friend,' I said. And my voice sounded strangely high-pitched.

'Aïcha.' My father repeated the name quietly, in stricken tones. Then he left.

He reappeared suddenly, startling me.

'Your mother and I arrange for you to go to all the best parties and social events. You have every opportunity to mix with people of your own class, our class. We've invested a great deal in you, Marie-Edwige!' His tone was angry now; he pointed a trembling finger at me. 'And all you do is mix with absolutely the wrong kind. First those grotesque acting lessons and now you're best friends with an Arab! Get a grip on yourself, Marie-Edwige, for heaven's sake!'

I remember looking him coldly in the eye, exactly as my drama coach, the legendary Jean-Laurent Cochet – onto whose programme I'd been accepted – had taught me. It was my turn to speak slowly now:

'My name is not Marie-Edwige, it's Alice.'

My father turned pale and left my room, slamming the door behind him so hard that my framed Greta Garbo poster fell off the wall.

★

Alice Larjac. The name of a customer at the boutique where I worked as a student, to earn the money for Cochet's classes. Until one day, when Cochet told me:

'Keep your money. You need it more than me. Life isn't going to be easy for you.'

There was nothing I could say. I accepted his generous offer. I joined the handful of students who attended his classes free of charge, and who never told the others. He was a great man. He taught almost all the greats of French cinema. I can scarcely picture Alice Larjac's face now: a dark-haired woman, elegant, smiling. I liked her name and made it mine without her ever knowing. Now I've made a reputation – and a decent living – for myself in the world of online coaching. I've never had an email from anyone called Alice Larjac asking why I have the same first name and family name as her. There are no Alice Larjacs to be found anywhere online, and yet she was a real person.

I continued law school without much conviction and threw myself into my drama classes with a passion. Aïcha and I were housemates now. My father wrote cheques, against his better judgement, so that I had enough to get by. Aïcha always found ways to make money – how, I don't want to know. We never talked about it. She was following her own brilliant path. She went to Sciences Po, graduated, got a place at the ENA – the training ground for elite executives and administrators. And then she met her boss. I can't give his name: he's one of the top company chiefs in the CAC 40. He was looking for a personal assistant. Someone to be always at his side and know all his business and take care of everything. Exhausting work, life in the fast lane. The perfect job for her. She's been his gatekeeper for years now. There's no way you can get to him without getting past Aïcha first. 'You'll have to check that with Aïcha...' A phrase he would utter several times a day.

Her boss is quite short, well below the average height for a man, and it bothers him. Plus, he's bald. Losing his hair at thirty seems to have affected him more than his height, or lack of it. Once, after an icy meeting during which two vast conglomerates (one of which was his) tore each other apart, the other big boss lost his rag and followed them out into the corridor towards the lifts. He called Aïcha's boss an upstart, a snake, and... *Mini-Me*. 'Mini-Me' stopped in his tracks and turned around to stare at the other man in silence. And then it all kicked off. Aïcha is taller than the average woman, and taller still in her heels. She's a stunner, and could be on the cover of *Vogue*. People stop talking when she enters a room. She took a step towards the other boss, he took a step back, and then all her old street talk came tumbling out, faster than Eminem in full flow. I can picture the scene. I've watched her tear a strip off kids in the street, even a dog once. A torrent of slang straight from the estates, peppered with American jive talk and Arabic. Three insults per sentence, a dazzling use of metaphor, comparisons that even the slang master-general Michel Audiard might have balked at. She smacked her chest with the flat of her hand, then pointed the finger at her accused. This was no tepid verbal joust; it was a white phosphorus bomb.

The other boss was left speechless, drained of colour, frozen to the spot. Aïcha and her boss turned back towards the lift.

'I know, I'm fired,' she said, dully.

'Not at all,' her boss replied. 'I'm doubling your salary.' And the lift doors slid shut.

My friend has been around the world about twenty times. She's shaken hands with Jeff Bezos, Roman Abramovich, even Donald Trump.

My journey was simpler. In fact, I'll admit my life was dull for about ten years. A series of relationships that went nowhere: either I left, or they left me. I loved the film world, but it did not love me. I loved the stage, but the stage did not love me either. I went to thousands of auditions, but got nothing, just a few crumbs. I wasn't bad, but clearly something was missing. And yet I saw plenty of half-baked girls get their breaks; they had all the charm and delivery of battered saucepans, articulating their words so badly that it was actually quite hard to make out what they were saying.

'That's just how it is, dear thing, the great unanswered riddle of our trade. Don't look for an explanation, you'll only get hurt,' Cochet told me.

I did commercials for insurance and washing powder. I took small roles in TV films, and on stage. A series, too. I had a small part, a cop who had reached the end of the line. Perfect timing. Because I'd reached the end of the line, too. I didn't have to work too hard to get into character.

Then one day, nothing. I called my agent, who said: 'We don't have anything at the moment, Alice, but we'll call you if something comes in.' My cash was running low. My father had stopped sending money. Aïcha was the only person keeping me afloat. She sent a transfer every month. One day, I told her I couldn't accept it any more. She took it badly:

'You're the most important person in my life. I wouldn't be where I am without you. I earn plenty: I can help you, no question. Think about what you might do. Who gives a fuck about TV and theatre any more? They're old news. Don't look back! Bardot and Belmondo? That's all finished. Your world is dead, meuf. Wake up!'

Aïcha's words were a shock to the system. She was right. It was never going to work. I stayed in bed for two days, letting it sink in. I felt dizzy. I was on a plane that was about to crash, preparing to leap into the void, unsure whether the weight on my shoulders was a backpack or a parachute. Could Alice Larjac be anything other than a stage name? Was there another Alice Larjac waiting to be discovered? There was. Aïcha made the case for it:

'You've slept with dozens of guys, you mix with the whole social spectrum, you've read hundreds of books, watched thousands of films, you've acted in plays, been to exhibitions, travelled… Now you need to do something with all of that!'

It was then that Aïcha placed the self-help book in my hands. I googled the author, followed her links, listened to podcasts, watched stuff on YouTube. It was a jungle out there. A vast, glittery Christmas market where everyone sold the same thing, with one or two variations — mostly just the name of the person selling the content. Male or female. A pretentious twat, or someone genuinely likeable. A tall, thin man, or a short, plump blonde woman. I spent two nights staring at all this, barely sleeping. I picked up the camera that my ex had left at my place when we broke up, the one I was meant to send him by post – with his watch. And I used it to film myself. I kept it simple to start with:

'Hi! I'm Alice and I'm going to talk about my break-up. Why things didn't work out between us, and why I left.'

Cochet's classes came flooding back. When I'd finished, I thought it was one of the best things I'd ever done. Better than the Enlightenment social satirist Marivaux; better than contemporary theatre; better than anything on TV, any commercial. Better than any of it.

At 3 a.m., I sat up in bed to take a look. I had 15,000 views and 200 comments. I read them all. By 2 p.m., I was up to 87,000 views and 2,500 comments. I went to the bookshop, bought twenty self-help books and thirty on sociology. I shut myself away for a week, filled a load of exercise books with notes, tried to see how what I was reading would fit with my own experience, with my life. And then I tried to go beyond my own experience, to understand how things might be for other people. I sent the camera and the watch back. I went out and bought my own equipment, and then I launched my YouTube channel with my second video: *If All Men Are Idiots then All Women Are Fools…*

And that's where I am right now. Aïcha's so proud of me, and she always comments on my videos. My parents are worried, but I'm totally over that now, and have been for a while. Of course, I don't see myself talking about male/female relationships on whatever's replaced YouTube in the metaverse when I'm sixty-four. But I can say one thing for sure: I feel at peace. I feel comfortable in my own skin.

I'm happy.

Yes, at this precise moment, I'm really happy.

She's been lying on the couch for a moment, and we still haven't spoken. She's playing with a Gauloise Blonde cigarette, passing it between the fingers of one hand without letting it fall. I slide the ashtray across to her, but she doesn't seem eager to light up.

'Who is Alice Larjac?'

'The woman who lives on the ground floor.'

'A woman who has changed her life.'

'Yes.'

'You're no longer taking photographs. Do you want to change your life, Nathalia?'

'Do you think the character is my double?'

'It's what you think that interests me.'

Silence falls once again. I should have liked her to say something in reply, but nothing comes. I'm sitting at my desk, looking at my collection. I collect only one thing, a very special type of key, made of wrought iron, known as a passepartout 'butterfly' or skeleton key. It has a characteristic design: two 'bits' are positioned back to back at opposite ends of the barrel, hence there's no flat top or 'bow'. The 'butterfly' is a ring with a heart-shaped attachment, fitted around the barrel, that slides from one end of the key to the other. If you block it against one of the 'bits', it forms the bow to be held in the hand, while the other end is inserted into the lock. The skeleton key was made by a master locksmith responsible for all the locks in a particular house. When the work was complete, he would present it to the head of the household, who was henceforth possessed of the only key capable of opening every door in the building. I bought my first piece from a little bric-a-brac shop a stone's throw from here. It amused me both for its symbolic value – a 'heart key' – and for its absolute practicality, its coherence of form and function.

'A collection begins with two pieces, when you find yourself looking for a third,' an antique dealer once warned me. That made me smile. I had bought a second passepartout key almost a year after the first, and I had indeed set about looking for a third one.

Since then, I have always seen that distinctive object as a symbol of my trade: a curious-looking key that includes the shape of a heart and opens dozens of doors. I value my small collection more than my professional archive. Last year, a learned association of lock enthusiasts asked me to write the catalogue preface to an exhibition of small, antique ironwork pieces. I found it tremendously difficult to write a short article which I hoped would be both informative and entertaining. And now I remember the celebrated author to whom I turned for help: I had searched online for anything and everything about… Sacha Guitry. His feeling for a turn of phrase, his love of a perfect, well-placed word, had been a great help to me that day. I was sadly unable to attend the opening of the exhibition. That same day, I was in Geneva for a conference on repression – a symptom of disarray, or a blessing in disguise? I was asleep for a good part of the proceedings and my neighbour, a Swedish analyst, had removed the earpiece connecting him to his interpreter a good while earlier and taken out a hip flask of rum which he offered me at regular intervals. Since I don't drink, it was only the intoxication of boredom to which I had succumbed.

I sit now, looking at my passepartouts arranged in a special order on my desk. Each heart has been slid to the centre of the barrel and turned to the right. How many doors could a passepartout open in a large eighteenth-century house? Fifteen? Twenty-five? I have nine in my collection. Nine times twenty-five… That's 225 doors waiting to be opened. Spread out over my desk, I have the means to open 225 doors. But those 225 doors have long ceased to exist. Reconstruction, revolutions and wars have destroyed all the locks they once opened, and now only the doors of the imagination remain.

Useless keys to doors that no longer exist. My collection. But I won't talk about that to Nathalia. It's she who has come here in search of a key, and I'm the one who can supply it. That's how I see it. That's how I've always seen it.

'What I see in your story, Nathalia, is your desire for a change of life. You would like a chain of events to fall into place that would lead you to become someone else. That would force you to take that decision, make that choice.

Except that, unlike in your story, life is not ruled by some kind of fate that deals the cards. In truth, your choices are simpler.'

'How do you know there's no such thing as fate, dealing the cards, as you put it?'

'It's a romantic notion, it's unrealistic.'

'How are my choices simpler?'

'Example of one simple choice that stems perfectly logically from your story: are you sure you want to continue with photography?'

I make time for silence, before going on. Questioning a patient's professional life is a delicate business, but it can be useful for the work of introspection. Analysis is all introspection, nothing else. And I continue:

'Are you sure there isn't another Nathalia, who might live a different life altogether? A little like the woman who wanted to be an actress but finally made a career as a self-help coach. With great success.'

Nathalia says nothing and I choose to take her silence as the start of a period of reflection on her own self.

This is our first session structured around the story-telling exercise. It seems to me that as a strategy for exchange, it's falling into place with interesting results. In a roundabout way, we are asking ourselves the right questions.

'There you are, then,' I say, as she pays me, 'now you need to work on this idea. In your own way.'

'Good. And you can work on this. In your own way.'

She hands me a scrap of paper on which she has written a telephone number.

'What's this?' I ask, intrigued.

'Alice Larjac's number, the one on her website. To book a coaching session. You two should talk. But you've already googled her. You know perfectly well she's for real.'

I stared at her. And I saw a brilliant, astonishing young woman. Frosty, perhaps, like her pale blue eyes. But fascinating, unpredictable. On her client sheet, I crossed out 'imagination, truth, mythomania', and wrote instead the only definition that seemed to fit. It took me a while to formulate it: dangerously disarming.

My patients' small obsessions, their manias, are strange but mostly harmless. My kleptomaniac regularly brought me things he'd 'spotted' in antique shops. He died last year, and I still have two pieces whose provenance I never succeeded in getting him to admit: an attractive paperweight made of cast iron, and an amadou wick lighter. In Nathalia's case, the scrap of paper with the telephone number is an unforeseen intrusion into my private world. It's a form of temptation. Quite unlike an old lighter kept in the back of a drawer.

Of course I checked if Alice Larjac was real. I found her website in a few clicks, and her videos on YouTube. She says nothing, anywhere, about her theatre training, nor about Jean-Laurent Cochet. She's reasonably well-versed in sociology, she reads widely, and she seems like a clever, intuitive girl. She does have long, brown hair, and she matches Nathalia's description of her in every other way. I hesitated at length, and then I called the number. I found myself talking to a man who booked me in for a telephone consultation on the day after next, at 4 p.m. I wanted to put it back to 6 p.m. He agreed and asked me to pay for the coaching session in advance, through the website. I did as instructed. Ninety euros for a twenty-minute conversation.

Two days later, the alarm on my mobile went off just after a patient had left. I switched it off, went to pour myself a Perrier, then sat in my armchair and punched in the number. A woman's voice answered this time, informing me that I was Bruno – the pseudonym I'd given when I signed up – and that I would be put through to Alice Larjac in less than a minute. Kitsch synthesizer music poured into my earpiece while I waited, then someone took the call.

'Hi Bruno, this is Alice, thank you for reaching out! How can I help you, Bruno?'

'Do you have a friend called Aïcha?'

Silence. Then the voice dropped to a lower register, to ask: 'You know Aïcha?'

'Rest assured,' I said, 'there's nothing suspicious about this call. I don't want to harm her in any way, nor you. Your question is my answer. I've paid for the coaching. We'll leave it there—'

'One more question,' she cut in. 'Who are you?'

Silence again, this time from me.

'I'm a shrink. I'm working with someone who knows you.'

'I won't ask who it is, and I'm sure you won't tell me. But that's interesting. Call me again someday, we can compare approaches. I'm sure we'd have an interesting conversation.'

'Perhaps… Goodbye, Alice.'

'Goodbye… Bruno.'

What I didn't tell Alice Larjac was that one of her talks had touched me quite deeply: *What Are You Up To?* The title of a short video, eight minutes long. According to her, you can tell how important you really are to the people who love you, by texting them this simple question. Someone who truly loves you will answer very quickly, in just a few minutes. Everyone has their phone to hand now; everyone checks it regularly, and listens out for the sound of a message alert. The other person will reply with whatever it is they're doing, before asking 'How about you?' The longer they take to reply to your light-hearted, affectionate question, the lower your importance in their eyes.

I texted my wife: WHAT ARE YOU UP TO? And again, to my daughter: WHAT ARE YOU UP TO?

My wife replied after four hours. 'I'm in the newsroom. Why?'

My daughter replied the next day. A plain and simple message: three question marks in a row.

The second envelope arrived this morning. Again by hand, which suggests to me that Nathalia lives close by. Doubtless she slips her envelopes into the letterbox in the main doorway of my building. We pay a company now, to distribute the post to each landing, take out the bins and clean the stairwells. We no longer have a concierge, and the old lodge has become a storage space for bikes, electric scooters and strollers.

I pull open the unsealed envelope: word-processed sheets. I push them all back inside. I'll read her narrative at about 3.30 p.m. Her appointment is at 4. I'm eager to see whose life she has slipped into this time, but I have some paperwork to shift before my first appointment this afternoon: my young anorexic, at 2 o'clock, who has deigned, at long last, to take a little grated carrot. We did a great deal of work on the colour orange, which we agreed to consider as essentially positive and friendly.

The telephone rings and I pick up. It's Catherine, my daughter. Of course, she wants to speak to her mother, who cannot be reached because she's at the newspaper, with her mobile going straight to voicemail. She doesn't even mention my WHAT ARE YOU UP TO?. I very quickly sense that she's bored with our conversation and wants to bring it to a close as rapidly as possible. To be fair, it was her mother she had hoped to reach here, not me. I want to tell her:

'You know, there's a girl I'm treating who's a little bit older than you. She's very beautiful, very brilliant. She likes me a lot, she writes me stories and I decode them.' But I'd never say anything of the kind to her.

As far as Catherine is concerned, I'm a doctor who never prescribes medicine. A father who juggles vague concepts and arcane texts, to treat male losers and female hysterics.

My poor, darling Cathy, if you only knew.

Before. That hallowed time, Before. Yes, Before, Catherine was an adorable little girl. I remember she loved the office, with its consulting couch. It was always, and remains, the quietest room in the apartment. She loved to lie flat on her stomach on the couch and apply herself to colouring in or drawing with her felt-tipped pens, with a diligence that never ceased to amaze me. It even worried me a little. I would say to her:

'Are you sure you're having fun, there?'

'Yes,' she would always answer. That 'yes'; the same firm, unqualified 'yes' as Nathalia.

Later, she would bring her homework, and apply herself to carefully forming As, Bs and Cs in scrolling, school script. Entire pages of letters, while I jotted personal notes in the margins of my patients' dossiers after listening to them all day.

A... A... A... a... a...

Slight increase in neurosis today. Defeatist tendencies.

Noticeable decrease in ticks. Has set a goal of travelling (unlikely).

B... B... B... b... b...

Off work for two months. Psychosis.

C... C... C... c... c...

Entering a phase of self-criticism, bordering on acute self-disparagement.

Sometimes I would sit her on my knee, and she would play with the objects arranged on my desk, in particular the passe-partout keys, of which there were fewer back then. I had still only collected three or four. She would manipulate the wrought-iron heart with nimble fingers, passing it from one end of the key to the other, and sometimes she would hide it behind her back and I would have to guess: which hand? Then, at the age of about twelve or thirteen, Catherine became closer to her mother, a process that has deepened over the years. Ending up where we are now, with the blank indifference that defines the few weekends she deigns to spend in our company.

I remember one Christmas – Catherine must have been about twenty-two or twenty-three. I went with her to the local garage, to sort out a problem with the insurance paperwork on her moped. Walking home, we passed a bric-a-brac shop. There, in the window, almost lost to sight amid an eclectic jumble of objects, was an eighteenth-century passepartout, with a heart.

'That key has your name on it!' said Catherine.

We went inside. The key was priced at forty-five euros. A derisory sum for an object of such quality. I thought I glimpsed an exchange of looks between my daughter and the shopkeeper, and so I said I'd think about it. I fancied that Catherine had come to an agreement with the man, and that she would come back later and buy it for me as a Christmas present.

I was wrong. I went back to the shop alone and bought it in January. I didn't even haggle over the price.

FIRST FLOOR

My name is Alban. I was always fat. Some people describe themselves, more delicately, as 'well covered', but I prefer to tell it like it is: fat. Already, in early childhood, I was a big, round blob. I remember my class at school. Funny things, classes of schoolkids. Always the same archetypes. As if each member of every set of twenty-five kids has a role to fulfil. Each one a cliché. It carries on, even in the army: take any platoon and you'd find the same mugshots as in your class at primary school.

The top of the class. Blond as a rule, and fair-skinned. He doesn't talk much, no one likes him, but everyone respects him. The class clown, at the opposite end, always in a gang with the other bottom-feeders, united in their mediocrity. The clown cracks jokes and entertains the girls, who feel sorry for him really. The top of the class is never normally friends with the second or third in line – no idea why. There's the shy one, often very thin, who never talks to anyone. The idiot, invariably ugly, always with a finger up his nose, never quite answering the question, grinning to himself. The tall one, always very dim, and goofy, but popular, like a dog that's missing a few brain cells but excellent at playing ball. The tall ones always like football. The sporty one, who starts shouting at the top of his voice when everyone comes out into the playground, and runs all over the place until he's exhausted. He plays ball with the tall one. The dreamer, who spends all his time staring out of the window or at his desk, as if there were things written there that only he can see.

The girls are easily sorted, in just three categories. There's the top of the class, with straight hair and braids, a face like a china doll and a careful, polished voice for reading out loud. She always gets top marks. She's a kind of brainiac, no one can understand anything she says; she's the teacher's pride and joy, and she refuses to have anything to do with her blond, fair-skinned male counterpart. And then there are the pretty ones and the ugly ones, with a broad spectrum in each category, ranging overall from the one who knocks you down dead, to the other who's just horrific. The beautiful one is some kind of angel, an angel who gets ordinary marks, no better or worse than any of the others, but she's beautiful. Just beautiful, that's all. She's the boys' first experience of feminine beauty: a little girl in their class, the pretty one. I think most of them spend the rest of their lives looking for her, without realising it. The ugly one is like a zero for bad behaviour, a splotch of ink on a carefully written dictation, a dollop of cold baked courgettes at the school canteen. Years later, you find out she's married, and you wonder how anyone could spend a night with her, let alone the rest of his life. Some kind of kamikaze. Whatever would he look like?

★

I forgot to list the most archetypal archetype of them all in that tiny microcosm: the fat one!

I was the fat one.

There's always a fat one everywhere: in a class of kids at school, at the office, at a drinks party, in a regiment, by the pool, on a chairlift at the ski resort, at a restaurant, in a train carriage, on the deck of a cruise ship, at a nightclub, round at your friends' place, in town: on land, at sea, in the air, there's always a fat one. We're everywhere. Omnipresent, we've always been here, and we will always be here. We are the mascot of the human race.

And only the human race. Take a herd of cattle – is there ever one cow much bigger and fatter than all the others? No. Same with a pack of wolves. Have you ever seen a pack with a wolf three times fatter than all the rest? Same with a litter of kittens, a herd of buffalo, a cage full of parrots, a hive, an anthill. You smile at my visual, observational humour, my clichéd group descriptions, and that's as it should be. Force of professional habit: I'm a cartoonist. A 'cartoonist and humourist', as my agent puts it. I have a strip in a well-known magazine: *M. Martin's Week*.

M. Martin is a character of my own invention. He's rather well covered too, and he reacts to the week's news and current events, anything from a tax increase to the president's latest speech, the death of a famous singer or a declaration of war. He goes everywhere with his dachshund, who always has a runny nose. The dog doesn't have a name. I honestly can't say why I drew the dog, just like that, one day. I've never had a dachshund, or any sort of pet.

In the first lockdown, my Instagram account went wild. People were shut up at home and they would ask me to do drawings. I did one a day, and I posted them online every evening at the same time. Messages and emojis would pour in, hundreds per second, on my phone.

As a rule, M. Martin reacts to four or five items of news. Martin is you, he's me, he's all of us. That's how I chose his name – it's the commonest surname in France, way ahead of Dupont, Durand or Moreau. The M. is anonymous, too. No one knows if it's the abbreviation for Monsieur, or the first letter of his first name. The superfans – the ones who film themselves online, talking in earnest detail about the latest strip, the latest book – all pronounce his name 'Em Martin.' But I just call him Martin, and I don't really understand why everyone's quite so wild about him. Recently in parliament, Fabien Roussel told the Minister of Finance that whenever he heard him speak, he felt like M. Martin, and started looking around for the dachshund!

My little character was such a success that my agent pushed me to publish albums of the collected strips. The first was a *Best of* the weekly cartoons, and the second was the first in a series called *The Daily M. Martin*. I wasn't keen on putting my hero into everyday situations, but the album sold so well that I'm now on to *The Daily M. Martin 4*.

My publisher has visions of a great classic – like Claire Bretécher's *Frustration*, or Philippe Geluck's *Le Chat*. Me, I was worried the formula would eventually wear thin, but my agent said:

'Dammit, Alban, we're fucking coining it, your guy and his dog are a once-in-a-lifetime hit!'

My agent's name is Sam. He's a sharp talker, which I never will be, and he sets publishers' and media bosses' heads in a spin. They'll agree to anything he says.

I'm a recluse in my apartment. My wife left five years ago, exactly at the time M. Martin was becoming a success. Like me, my wife was... I was going to say fat, but no, she was well covered. There it is, that's the appropriate term, that's what suits her. In fact, she resembled a Renoir. A late-period Renoir, with the skin a little too pink, and the mouth too red, the features a bit blurry, a bit scribbled. True, the master's hands were paralysed with rheumatism at the time. That was my wife, a late Renoir. And that made me sad. Because the truth is, I like thin girls. Tall, very slim blondes. The kind you see sunbathing down south, their skin all golden and salty, their little pointy breasts nestled in tumbling tresses of hair bleached by the sea. That's my type. Trouble is, I'm not their type. That's not very *feminist*, not very *politically correct*, is it? If Sam was here, he'd write: 'Fucksake, man, don't send this to anyone! If you come out with crap like that in an interview, I'll have heart failure. You'll have the death of your best buddy on your conscience!'

On the afternoon in question, I'd gone for a walk in the Jardin du Luxembourg. It was mid-July, and the heavy, clammy heat of a Parisian summer had settled on the streets. I'd done the first sketches for my weekly strip, and I was waiting for the news on BFM TV to get it finished. I was torn between the Tour de France, the latest provocative statement from a shock-merchant on TV, and a financial scandal that left me cold. I had gone out for a change of scene, to clear my head. I was pouring sweat, and my XXXL T-shirt was sticking to me. All around me, in the gardens, guys were roasting in the sun, bare-chested. I'd have done the same, but I'd have looked like a beached whale reclining by the water. The heat was unbearable. I thought to myself that they should air-condition the entire city. Perhaps that could be the final drawing in the strip. M. Martin would go out for a walk in air-conditioned Paris, and then he would rail at the government for taking away the sun. Something like that. And the dachshund's nose drip would stop running. I was exhausted. I sat down at the park kiosk. At that moment, I never thought that this one simple act would change my life.

The waiter brought me a Get 27 – a mint liqueur on ice. For a few minutes, it brought my body temperature down to something like normal. I felt I might combust in the heat. The cooling effect of the Get soon wore off, and I ordered another. That was when she sat down: tall, blonde, thin, very attractive, suntanned. She was wearing a white outfit with buttons at the front, and sky-blue trainers. Strangely, her figure reminded me of something. What was her name, that girl, last summer? Jenny. Yes, that was it. I'd met her at Sam's, in Saint-Tropez: 'My wife's bringing a friend, sex mad, you can have some fun!' I'd resented his implication that I stood my best chance with a desperate sex addict. I looked carefully at the blonde woman. It wasn't Jenny. Then her face shot out from the depths of my memory like the fizz from a Coke can that's been shaken too hard. It was Vanessa. Vanessa…

Vanessa… Vanessa Valière. Voilà!

We'd been at high school together. When was it? The last two years? No, she wasn't there for the final exams; it must have been the two years before that. Two years. Two years spent staring at her, because she was beautiful then, too. She was very beautiful now. At school she would turn on the charm to get me to write her essays on Montaigne – and I did. I wasn't stupid. I knew all those coy smiles, all that hair-flicking wasn't really for me, but for the top marks I could deliver.

Men are cowards. They'd rather be with a Barbie who pretends to flirt than be on their own. It flatters them, fires their imagination: for a few seconds, they think it's all for them, and that makes them happy for a day. And girls of that age, they love to try out their charms on pathetic guys they don't really want. There's no danger in it; they feel safe. I remember the guy who used to come and wait for her outside the school gate. He was tall, very lean, very chic, a bit older than us. He had a dirt bike. I remember the day she broke into a run and threw herself into his arms. A stunning vision. Stunning, yet terrible. The long, lean guy with his motorbike, and the fat one, clutching a Bounty bar. No competition. Not even a losing battle. Alpha and omega.

She seems to be looking around for someone. I almost want to walk over and say hello. I could tell her about myself, what I'm doing now, tell her that I am M. Martin. She would cry out in surprise, and then she'd say: 'That's amazing! Alban, it's really you! Unbelievable!' It's a familiar scenario, a technique I often use to fish for praise and compliments. But right now I'm too anxious to move because I know what will happen next. I can feel it: a tall, lean guy will arrive – the person she's waiting for. And by his thinness alone, his line, his fluid grace, he will dissolve my fragile dreams. Just like when I was sixteen years old, all over again. It's a nightmare from which I can never wake up.

And here he comes now. She smiles. He's tall, he's lean, blond, very elegant, very handsome. Almost too good-looking, borderline queer. Like David Bowie in *Absolute Beginners*... No, more like the video for 'Let's Dance', when he plays the Australian boss in a designer suit telling off a young Aboriginal worker. That's it, spot on. Men really do fall into identifiable categories: stylish blonds like Bowie; small, dark, nervy types like Nicolas Sarkozy; salt-and-pepper charmers like George Clooney; fat boys like me. Clearly, she prefers the Bowie lookalikes. Tall blonds are her type.

I feel sick at the thought. I order another Get 27.

Back at my place, I scribble the end of my strip about the air-conditioned city. It's not great. But I don't want to listen to the news, and I can't focus on work just now.

In bed later, I'm plagued with nonsensical dreams I won't even remember in the morning. And the suffocating heat. I try everything: on top of the blanket, no blanket, between the sheets, no sheets, on the floor, with the fan on, the window open. Nothing works. The heat is omnipresent; it's inside me.

I feel as if my body has absorbed the heat of the sun, that it will never recover its normal temperature. In the morning I make myself an iced coffee, then I scan through my piece before sending it to the editor.

Vanessa Valière. I punch her name into my phone and do a picture search, with no luck. It seems she's on LinkedIn and Facebook, but both accounts are private. At last, I find a public Instagram account: Vanessa Valière @Vanouval.

I see posts of her in her neighbourhood. The bistro features quite often. There are pictures of her in the Seychelles, too. Never with a guy. No kids, either. My mobile rings and the pictures disappear, leaving a name on the screen: Sam.

'What are you doing? Don't forget our album – we have to get it in by the deadline, in time for it to come out in September.'

Sam always dispenses with the preliminaries, gets straight to the point.

I tell him I'm looking for a girl's address online. And that I can't find it.

'Who's the meuf?'

'Just a meuf.'

'Does the meuf have a name?'

'Of course she has a name. I know what she does, she's on Facebook, Instagram, everywhere. But no clue as to her private address.'

'I'll find it. Send me her name, her job, her Insta.'

★

My phone rings fifteen minutes later. It's Sam.

'Eighteen, Rue de la Pentille, in the fifteenth.'

'How'd you do that? There's nothing online.'

'I called her work, said I was delivering an Amazon parcel. Told them I was out on the street, that I didn't have the door code, and she wasn't answering her mobile.'

'And they believed you...'

'Of course they fucking believed me. They said: "You're sure you're on Rue de la Pentille? Number eighteen?" People are bloody ignorant apes, Alban. Now get back to work.'

I've been in position at the bistro for two hours. From the terrace, I can see the entrance to her building. She'll be along soon – people are coming home from work. She has some high-ranking post in a 'strategic communications consultancy'. Smoke and mirrors to extract big bucks from rich bosses in exchange for two or three pieces of common-sense advice.

Here she is. She appears around the corner of the street, walking quickly, her phone wedged against her ear. She's smiling. She's going to walk right past me.

'At Luna's tonight?' she says. 'Hmm... All right, then... Ha!' And she giggles.

She's walked on by. She presses a code into the keypad, opens the door. It's all over. No, it's not all over. This is only the beginning.

I've spent my whole day sitting with a glass in front of me, waiting. I loathe nightclubs and hipster bars, but here I am chez Luna. I stare at the great, golden moon that hangs in the centre of the restaurant, beneath the mezzanine bar. Around me, everyone is smiling, and this happiness incenses me. The carefree attitude, the money, the girls. They're all good-looking, hip, happy. I want to redraw every one of them, with Martin's dachshund's head and his runny nose. In one corner, at the noisiest table, I spot the well-known presenter of a programme watched nightly by the whole of France – or a fair portion of France at least. He's surrounded by a crowd of people, joking and laughing out loud. I pray he doesn't see me – he's been pestering Sam for months to get me on his show. I have a horror of interviews: they scare me and, what's more, I'm terrible at them.

Damn. He's seen me. Now he's gesturing for me to join them all. I don't move, and so he gets up and walks over, smiling broadly.

'How's it going? Has Sam been in touch about the show? We've been waiting to hear from you, it would be great to have you on, introduce you, put you out there...'

'We'll see,' I tell him. I sound blasé.

'Are you waiting for someone? Come and wait with us! Is she hot?' he adds, laughing. I tell him I was about to leave. He looks disappointed, then quickly shakes it off.

'Up to you – you're very welcome to join us, anyway, and even more welcome on the show. Ciao, Alban!' He slaps me on the shoulder and goes back to his table.

I order another Get 27. The DJ's hypnotic beat is lulling me into a stupor when a svelte blonde presence enters my field of vision: Vanessa. She's out with friends. Two girls, two men. No sign of David Bowie. They're all laughing together, too. They look happy, like all the others. No doubt they'll join the TV star's table and this whole farce will erupt in a gale of laughter. The Get 27s are going to my head. What the fuck am I doing here? I no longer know, but nor do I care. I'll let myself be carried along.

'Follow that car.'

The taxi driver stares at me in the mirror, amused. The party continued late into the evening. One of the guys – the blond, obviously – had been coming on strong to Vanessa, and now she's getting into a car with him. Leaning in towards my driver, I can see them silhouetted between the headlights. She's kissing him. I'm sure they're going back to her place.

My taxi stops at the top of the street. I see them get out, hear them laughing. She kisses him again as they sway gently in the entrance to the building. Then she pushes the door.

I get out of my taxi and walk towards the front of the building. A light is sure to come on. There, on the second floor. They're going to make love all night long, and here am I, standing outside on the street. Something surges inside me, like a bulldozer revving to the max up a gentle slope. It's not hatred. No, it's a sense of injustice.

It should be me up there with her, in her apartment, me behind the bright, translucent drapes, me on her sofa, me in her bed. I stand on the sidelines of life. I walk the hard shoulder of life's motorway. And it's been that way for a very long time.

Suddenly, right here and now, I want to die. I want it all to end. I want to kill myself.

I walk the streets, and the cool night breeze turns my thoughts of suicide to thoughts of revenge. Revenge. I will take my revenge and kill myself at the same time. Two birds with one stone. She likes tall-thin-elegant blonds, which leaves me only one solution. I'll kill the fat guy and release my thinner self. I'll murder the man who's poisoned my life for as long as I can remember. And as I walk, already, it seems he's no longer there. I see myself in my mind's eye – thin, svelte. The process has begun. It's unstoppable now, irreversible. I no longer feel fat.

Already, I am no longer that man.

Dr Sirup was about sixty, thin and gaunt, with white, wire-brush hair and small, steel-rimmed spectacles. His physique contrasted singularly with his name, which conjured images of pink-white marshmallows or Turkish delight dusted with icing sugar. But he was a comforting presence. There was something therapeutic in his dry manner and his bolt-upright hair. After a consultation lasting an hour and a half, I left with a prescription as long as the receipt for my monthly shop in the Monoprix food hall. I had refused to enter a clinic. The very thought of finding myself with a multitude of fat people in hospital beds made me feel quite sick, and anyway, I had drawings to deliver.

My usual port-and-Bounty aperitif was a thing of the past. No more deep-fried spring rolls at Ming's. No more T-bone steaks at Marcel's. No more fruit juice with sugarcane syrup, no more sugar in my morning coffee, no more Coke, ice-cream, sorbet, jellied fruit... From now on, I was running on two bowls of disgusting soup a day, a paper-thin steak, a knob of butter, an apple, an apricot, a clementine, a bulb of fennel, and six sets of three pills every three hours, with a large glass of water. Eight vials of liquid, two sachets of yellow powder, two energy bars, a cardiac stimulant, an anti-fatigue supplement, two muscle relaxants, a sleeping pill, soluble vitamins, an anxiolytic. I went to the pharmacy to procure the essential hardware for this commando assault on my own body: a set of scales.

'It's a Swedish model – ultra-precise, with a very ergonomic design. It will take up to three hundred kilos,' the pharmacist reassured me. I would stay indoors, and see no one, for several months.

Sunday, 11 August

Four weeks and a day since I started my diet. Dr Sirup's programme is delivering. I've lost eleven kilos – almost two clothes sizes. He tells me to pay careful attention to the acceleration phase. Sam called, and my publisher. They asked me out to dinner. I refused. I'm staying shut up at home. The magazine strip was a hit. No other news.

Monday, 16 September

Sirup's 'acceleration phase' has been and gone. I've been to see him six times since the start of the diet. He's satisfied with my progress. He tells me that soon, I can start training at the gym. It's incredible how much I've lost! My clothes are hanging off me. I had to go to the Levi's store for a new pair of jeans. When I look at my old clothes hanging in the wardrobe – some of them over fifteen years old – I feel I'm living in someone else's house.

Thursday, 10 October
I began training at a gym ten days ago. It's exhausting. But impressive. My body is changing shape – completely. There's a dedicated coach for guys like me, but the others just work out for the fun of it.

Tuesday, 12 November
Sirup is very pleased with my results. 'Not as pleased as me,' I told him. I no longer feel the urge to eat rich food. I'm eating a little more than I did at first, and I'm on new pills. I'm great friends with Stéphane, a gay guy who works out manically to please his boyfriend.

Monday, 16 December
The scales tell me I've lost 42 kilos. They keep a record. Another 10, a few more trips to the gym, and I'll be just right.
    I invited Stéphane over for a drink. I see no one socially at the moment, so his visit was a welcome change. He's charming. He reads *M. Martin's Week* and is delighted to have met me. I gave him an original, signed strip. Sam leaves messages. He's worried that he hasn't seen me. I reassure him. If the drawings keep landing on the editor's desk, and if they still make the fans laugh, then I must be doing all right.

Thursday, 2 January

Voilà. It's over. Sirup will see me for check-ups over the coming months. He read me a complex report on my blood and cardiac test results. Everything's fine. I went straight home after the consultation. Stéphane no longer comes to the gym, and we didn't exchange numbers. I may never see him again. I'm going to bin this journal. It's not mine. It's someone else's story now.

Now, I'm looking at myself in the bathroom mirror.

Tall. I never thought of myself as this tall. Thin, svelte, remarkably ripped. Time to reopen the case on Vanessa. One last detail requires attention: my look.

Pearl-grey jacket: 2,500 euros.

Levi's 501s: 130 euros.

Black lace-up brogues: 400 euros.

White shirt: 220 euros.

Venetian cufflinks: 140 euros.

Shampoo, cut, blond rinse, blow-dry: 180 euros.

Steel Rolex Oyster Perpetual (in place of my green Swatch): 5,700 euros.

Never before have I splashed so much cash in a single afternoon. I realise now that I never spent much on myself before. The polite respect that my new-found thinness inspires is quite fascinating. When I entered the Rolex boutique, wearing my grey jacket, with my impeccable haircut and athletic physique, I was greeted with instant deference. If I'd stepped into any such place six months before, with my worn-out jeans and T-shirt, and the girth of a hot-air balloon, I would have stood waiting for twenty minutes or more before anyone served me.

I'm on the other side now.

I'm sitting on the bistro terrace. It's cold. An icy wind nips at my face. The last time I was here, I was fat, and the tarmac was melting in the heat. Six months. I order a Perrier. Vanessa should be along soon, turning the corner of the street. I shall stop her:

'Hello! I'm sorry, it's Vanessa, isn't it? Vanessa Valière? Alban Charvier – we were at school together.'

'Alban… Oh my goodness. No way!'

She'll be amazed. She won't recognise me, and I'll do my thing – the guy who's made it, with his almost-cult daily cartoon strip. Volume 5 of *The Daily M. Martin* is almost out. Sam is bombarding me with messages. He insists on seeing me tomorrow. He won't be disappointed.

Perhaps she got home just before I pitched up at the bistro. The thought has tormented me for the past half-hour and more. She's at home and I'm out here like an idiot on the café terrace. Perhaps she isn't going out tonight. I could come back tomorrow. But I need to see her. I'm going to buzz her apartment. I'll say I saw her going into the building. My thinness and elegance have made me bold. I can do anything now.

Faced with the keycode panel, I dry up. I'd forgotten about that part. Fortunately, there's a button marked CONCIERGE. I'm saved. A little grey-haired woman opens the main door.

'Yes?'

'I've come to see Mademoiselle Valière and... silly of me, I know, I've quite forgotten the code,' I tell her, with my most charming smile.

'But Mademoiselle Valière doesn't live here any more,' says the little grey-haired lady.

I gaze at her for a few seconds. I can hear my breathing and the beat of blood in my temples.

'I'm sorry?' I say, at last, with a gasp.

'She left... Five months ago. She got married in Brazil. She said she'd send me her new address, but nothing's come so far.'

'But that's impossible... Impossible... It's impossible...' I repeat the words over and over, like a madman, like a stuck record.

'Well no, monsieur... She's not here...'

I slap the palm of my hand hard against the stone façade and break down, sobbing uncontrollably.

'There now, monsieur, don't take it so hard! She was a pretty girl, Mademoiselle Valière, but there'll be others... A fine-looking man like you...'

I look at her, with tears in my eyes. The little grey-haired lady is gazing at me with a kind, gentle expression.

One month later, I met Patricia on the set of the show fronted by the well-known TV presenter and watched by the whole of France, on which I finally consented to appear. She's a make-up artist. She's not especially slim, nor blonde, nor tall. She's sweet, gentle, funny, and I adore her. We are very much in love.

'So you called Alice Larjac?'

'Perhaps. Perhaps not. Are you disappointed?'

'Disappointed at what?'

'That I may not have called her.'

'No, because I don't believe you.'

I had a strange dream last night. I found myself in a corridor whose height, width and length were impossible to tell.

I stood before a heavy door and realised that I had no key. And the longer I stood there, the greater my need to open the door. I searched my pockets. Nothing. This was a key I was meant to have, in my dreamworld, but it wasn't there.

And then I turned around. At the other end of the corridor, far away, I saw Nathalia. She was holding my collection of keys in both hands. I looked back at the door: it was standing ajar. I pushed it and found myself gazing out over a silent, desert landscape of infinite beauty. Before me lay an oasis of luxuriant vegetation. I heard the murmur of pure, fresh water. An avenue of trees led to a cool spring. It was guarded along its length by dogs lying on the ground, each a short distance apart, their snouts pointing forward between their paws, like quiet sentinels. I woke up.

All morning, I played three words over in my mind: key, door, woman. Door-key-woman. But what is a door-key-woman? Where had the oasis and its gentle canine guard sprung from? Psychoanalysis sometimes follows trails guided by wordplay; it has blind alleys too.

'Why must one "believe", Nathalia? Or rather, what should one believe?'

'I should be believed. Me.'

'You?'

'Yes.'

'I like the way you say "Yes". Depressed people rarely say yes in that tone of voice.'

I say nothing more. I look at her. There's something strange about Nathalia: once she's left the room, I find myself unable to picture her face. When I try to call her to mind in the days that follow, her image is blurred, as if she is standing behind a pane of frosted glass. All I see is a kind of unfocused aura. Yesterday evening, I told my wife about the phenomenon, and her answer was disconcerting, to say the least:

'Perhaps she doesn't exist.'

'Whatever do you mean?'

'I don't know...' she murmured, and then she fell asleep.

I lay awake for hours, turning the mysterious phrase over and over. She doesn't exist. It was absurd, even funny, I decided, at length. I pictured Nathalia as an angel, an elf, an ectoplasm materialised from who knows where. It seemed clear to me that there was only one logical conclusion: I was going mad.

Whereas in fact I'm perfectly lucid, and the cash Nathalia pays me is very real.

I lean forward just slightly, imperceptibly. I look at the lashes outlining her blue eyes, her pale complexion and the perfect symmetry of her features. How could I forget the face of such a beautiful young woman?

'Were you in love as a teenager?'

'Yes.'

'With a boy who didn't notice you?'

'Yes, but I found him again later, and I had a relationship with him.'

'Because you still loved him?'

'No, for revenge.'

'Go on…'

'To do what I should have done at the time.'

'To put things in order?'

'Exactly.'

'What happens when things aren't in order?'

'Disorder. Disarray.'

'Is your life in disarray?'

'Yes.'

'Are we putting things in order, here?'

'I think so.'

'Why a cartoonist?'

'That's his job.'

'In your story.'

'In real life.'

'I know he exists. I checked online. There are very few pictures of him. He's a thin man.'

'He's real.'

'Like Alice Larjac?'

'Yes.'

'They all exist?'

'All of them.'

'And you know all about their lives?'

'Yes.'

'The afternoon at the Luxembourg. The meeting with an old classmate. How is that possible?'

'He threw his newspaper into a park bin. I fished it out.'

I find myself wondering if I've ever been caught out. Invariably, Nathalia has an answer for everything. My counter-arguments shatter against the wall of her implacable logic. Usually, my patients grumble and complain; they put up a fortress of lies, certain that I won't fall for it – like children caught misbehaving who invent the most extraordinary tales to avoid being kept behind after school. When will the patients on the couch all understand that I'm not here to mete out punishment? Nathalia has understood: if I tried to give her detention, she would play truant, proud and insolent.

'Did you struggle with your weight as a teenager?'

'Yes.'

I'm relieved to hear this because I'm almost certain Nathalia is making her stories up. She tells me, calmly and logically, that all her characters are real, but she is talking about herself through their stories. My strategy is working.

She pays me, and hands me a coloured card.

'What's this?'

'An invitation. To a book signing.'

★

She has left. I look at the coloured card and am unable to suppress a smile. Then I look across at the couch. Nathalia… I try to picture her face, but once again, all I see is a blur. Only one or two remarkably precise details come to me: her eyes, her eyelashes, the curve of her ears, the dimple at the corner of her lips, on the left, which is without its twin on the right. A fragmented image, as if she were bending over a mirror that lies shattered on the ground. Details of her face appear in the shards. The analyst is a mirror of sorts, in which the patient sees their own self.

That being so, why am I broken into pieces?

I stand in line in the bookshop. The cartoonist is sitting behind a desk piled with copies of his album *The Daily M. Martin*. Next to him sits a dark-haired man who stands up when his telephone buzzes and goes outside to take the call. Soon, it's my turn. Alban is tall, thin, elegant. I hand him my copy of the book. He smiles and asks me my first name. I tell him, and then I ask for a dedication, in the name of a woman who is not my wife.

'It's for Vanessa.'

'I knew a Vanessa once,' he says with an enigmatic smile, as he pens a small drawing of his character, and the dachshund.

'Oh, really? It's a popular name...' I say.

'Yes,' he agrees, 'very.'

He hands me back my copy. Already a young woman has taken my place and is asking him for a selfie. I've extracted no new information. I feel the urge to ask someone if Alban was ever fat – that's why I'm here, after all. A woman in her fifties is leafing through her signed album.

I walk over.

'Monsieur Martin has quite a fan club!' I venture awkwardly.

'*Em* Martin,' she corrects me. 'Yes, I like his work a lot.

He's one of very few who really make me laugh – like Voutch, and Sempé. Alas, Sempé is no longer with us, of course.'

'Alas indeed.'

A silence settles between us, so I go on:

'Have you been reading him for long?'

'I've got all his albums, since the beginning. How about you?'

'Almost all of them… But… He was much, er, weightier before, wasn't he?'

She gives a small, sad smile, then lowers her voice, confidentially.

'I think so too. The first albums were so funny, and you're right, they did seem weightier, more impactful. Especially in lockdown, when he did a drawing for his fans every day. But he's getting repetitive now, I find. I still buy the books, though… Like you.'

She moves away to talk to the young girl who took the selfie, who's waving to her. 'Weighty' rather than outright 'fat'. A textbook Freudian slip. I feel like patting myself on the back – it's been a while since I heard such a classic example, and from my own mouth. A modicum of self-analysis tells me that deep down inside, I don't want to know if what Nathalia writes is the truth, or fiction. Why is that?

I emerge onto the street. The dark-haired man, Alban's sidekick, is still outside the bookshop, talking into his phone. I can hear what he's saying:

'What the fuck? You never sign that kind of contract, what the hell's come over you? Those terms are for beggars, not choosers…'

It seems that Sam the agent, at least, is real enough.

*

I dropped the album into a bin on my way home. How could I have explained the dedication – to me and someone called Vanessa – to my wife?

SECOND FLOOR

I have the best job in the world: I write song lyrics. Pretty phrases, rhymes, couplets, refrains. All contained on a single sheet of paper. I sign my name at the bottom: Vincent Véga.

Plenty of people try their hand at what I do, but very few succeed. I'm one of the ones who have. I've written huge hits, and less-well-known songs. One or two flops, too. Most importantly, I make a living out of it. Today, I've dried up. My page is almost blank. I can't find a rhyme for 'girl', in a very sophisticated song, for a very hip artist. It's about an 'escort girl', wandering and lost on the streets of London. She emerges from her client's place and wonders if her life is going the right way.

Men have taken advantage of her body, her beauty, her naivety. She's been used, and she knows that now. She's a victim. Beautiful, and a victim.

'That's the message you've got to get across, Vince, and you're the best in the business.' The producer's praise sounded like a warning. I listened to Jane Birkin's 'Lolita Go Home', trying to get some inspiration for the street-walking, but I'd have done better to leave the record on the shelf. Now Gainsbourg's catchy melody is banging about in my head, with Jane Birkin's breathy vocals, around and around between my ears.

Girl.... Girl... Curl... Furl... Pearl....
Pearl... A string of pearls?
Raindrops like a shower of pearls?
A shower of pearls like rain?
My life's pearl?
I'm an escort, escort girl
My life, a pearl?
Shattered, chic
Mother of Pearl...

Pffft. It's terrible. Mother of Pearl... Where the hell did *she* come from? I cross it all out. Belphégor opens one eye. A poet's cat is like a witch's familiar, as everyone knows. Cocteau, Colette, Baudelaire all said so before me. But their indolence has something annihilating about it. Try watching a sleeping cat and then getting any work done. Then come and tell me what you think!

We go back a long way, Belphégor and I. Eleven years this year. I found him one morning in Parc Montsouris, very tiny, very much abandoned, mewing fit to burst. I took him home and poured him the dregs of a carton of milk, after which we shared a tin of tuna that provoked a great show of purring and love. A gleaming black silhouette formed itself into a ball in the middle of the bed, forcing me to arrange my body in a zigzag under the sheets so as not to disturb 'the cat'. This went on for several years and is the reason for my scoliosis, which regularly flares up. I explained my puss-in-bedclothes problem to the radiologist, who told me:

'I have the same problem with my python.'

I was reassured. There were others out there crazier than me. On the morning after that first night, with no songs to write for anyone, I got through plenty of ink and paper nonetheless, which Belphégor took great delight in clawing to shreds, when he wasn't patting at the nib of my pen.

I was trying to find a name. I wrote long lists, each dumber and duller than the last, from Mew-mew to Deep Purr-ple, Kitty-Kat and (Black) Treacle. At last, after pages of crossings-out, the obvious name appeared: Belphégor. Genius. Like a struck match, the name illuminated the dim passages of my televisual culture. Belphégor the cat was born. Like the phantom that stalked the galleries of the Louvre in the legendary black-and-white TV series of years gone by, he was swathed all in black, with bright, piercing eyes. Belphégor had risen.

'It's a female.'

'What do you mean, a female? Absolutely not, it's a male and his name is Belphégor.'

'No. Nope...' the vet shook his head, 'I can tell a tom cat from a female. She can only be about a month-and-a-half old.'

Belphégor stared at me, unsettled by the vet's palpations all over his body – stomach, teeth, paws, claws, fur… And what about the name? What use was it now, the genius name I'd found? I'd have to start all over again, take out my pen and rack my brain for hours before settling on Kittywinkle, or Tiggy-wiggy.

'Anyway, Belphégor's a perfect name,' said the vet. 'Belphégor's a woman, in the TV series – in fact, it's Juliette Gréco.'

'Juliette Gréco?'

'Yes, the Phantom of the Louvre turns out to be Juliette Gréco under hypnosis. She's in the power of a bizarre character who claims to be the head of the Rosicrucian cult. François Chaumette plays the part. Great actor. He disguises her in the black cape and mask to cover his own tracks: he's after a mysterious alchemical compound made by the Renaissance scientist Paracelsus and hidden inside a statue in the museum. But then a student – played by Yves Rénier in his first television role – ruins all his plans. He's investigating the mystery of Belphégor, and he falls under Gréco's spell.'

I must have been staring at him open-mouthed because he added proudly:

'I'm a bit of a film and TV buff. Any other questions?'

I hadn't found the success I know now, back then. I was living in a tiny apartment near Parc Montsouris, and my romantic conquests were vanishingly rare. My dreams, and my songs, tended to put girls off. They say women prefer artists and dreamers; I'm here to disprove that particular theory. Over and above a certain age, the female of the species likes a man who can offer security, comfort, money, a future. As for me, I could offer nothing of the kind. Just me, myself and I – and that was never good enough.

At a party or a dinner with friends, a girl might find me funny, sweet, nice, but nothing more. Belphégor, on the other hand, shared all my fears and anxieties, all my dreams. Success came with 'G for Girl', the first single from a young female singer called July Mira, recorded in the unlikely setting of a cellar fitted out as a studio, in Aubervilliers. Never again would I see such unalloyed enthusiasm as from the small team that put the song together.

I had met July Mira in a café on Place Saint-Michel. It's no longer there. I liked the way she looked, with her short hair, her sexy clothes, her tomboy style. But my approach fell at the first hurdle when she told me, very sweetly, that she liked girls. In fact, she was waiting for her girlfriend, Murielle, a songwriter.

A few hours later, the three of us were in Murielle's studio listening to a demo. The tune was catchy, but they felt something was wrong with the opening words. I suggested I write some lyrics. 'G for Girl'.

The song was a big hit, and an album was planned, when Murielle and July split up, shattering both their careers with a single blow. But not mine. Pascal Nègre, the boss of Universal Music, insisted on meeting the writer of this flash-in-the-pan hit. I wrote an album for him that never took off. But my lyrics made the rounds, from cocktail party to late-night drinks, demo artist to arranger… and the doors to my songwriting career were flung open.

Success had come quickly, in the end. Just as soon as Belphégor entered my life. My lucky black cat. I met Clotilde at Universal, around the time of 'Pale-eyed Girl' (No. 3 in the charts for seven weeks). She was an assistant in Artists & Repertoire back then. Today, she's artistic director, though artistry is less her concern than sheets of figures and concert dates... But far be it from me to speak ill of my beloved wife.

We married very quickly. Perhaps we'd been waiting for one another just that little bit too long. We had Bruno the following year. He's seven now, an adorable little boy who loves his mama best, like all little boys. I only write the songs, so it's easy to wriggle out of the worst of our business – the endless arranging sessions, TV promotions, touring, foreign travel. All I need for work is a pen, a sheet of paper, a melodic line... And Belphégor. I'm hardly ever asked to give interviews, and when I do, I never know what to say; so I talk about her, which makes for a very short interview indeed, because the editors invariably cut all the stuff about cats. I had just about managed to reconcile my sedate, married life with all the sequins and glitter, when everything began to fall apart.

Bruno developed a cough. Clotilde and I thought it was a touch of flu, but then the whistling and whining in his chest alarmed us. We took him to our family doctor, a brilliant medic, passionate about French chanson – I think that's why I chose him, truth be told. He gave us his diagnosis: a tendency to asthma. Then he asked whether anything might be triggering it.

'What do you mean, triggering it?' I asked.

'Dust, flowering plants, I don't know... Cats?'

'Cat hair? Belphégor...' said Clotilde straight away.

'I'm sorry?' said our doctor.

'That's our cat's name. Well, my husband's cat's name. But she's always been with us.'

'Yes, absolutely. I've had Belphégor since forever,' I added, perhaps a little too firmly.

'Well, in that case...' said our doctor, slowly.

He prescribed medicine and inhalers for Bruno. We should wait to see if the cough improved. Perhaps it was psychosomatic?

'Pyscho what?'

'Somatic... Nervous. Due to stress, if you prefer. Pressure at school? Trouble with his classmates, a bad mark. At that age...'

'My son's never had any problems like that. Have you, sweetheart?' said my wife to Bruno, who squirmed in his chair.

'No, I don't have problems,' he confirmed.

The subject appeared closed, but my wife was not about to leave matters there. The inhalers helped a little, but Bruno still coughed from time to time. It didn't bother me much, but Clotilde treated it with the utmost seriousness. And she was right – asthma is a serious business. She took Bruno to see the head of the pulmonary department at the Hôpital Pompidou, who prescribed new drugs and a blood test for cat dander.

'What the hell is cat dander?' I asked my wife when she reported back.

'Cats lick themselves, and when they do, they release stuff into the air, which evaporates, and it can trigger asthma.' At least one of us had listened to the doctor.

'So why aren't I asthmatic?' I asked. 'Or you, for that matter? Huh? Why? Why has everything been fine until now?'

'Don't get so worked up, we just need to know about it, and that's that.'

That was that when the blood test results came back. Bruno was seriously allergic to cat hair. Or dander. The doctor's advice was categorical.

I went along with Clotilde and Bruno this time.

'I'm afraid you'll have to consider parting company with your cat,' said the doctor, by way of a greeting.

'Out of the question!' My voice rang out sharply across the austere consulting room.

'Your son is allergic, monsieur. His asthma is likely to get worse... He is very prone to attacks, and on top of everything else, you smoke.'

I stared at him in astonishment.

'I can smell it,' he said, with the smile of a professor of medicine who brooks no disrespect.

Back at our apartment, I shut myself in my office, where Belphégor lay waiting. She stretched and walked across to roll on my papers, gazing at me with loving eyes. Even the thought of parting company...

Several years ago, I wanted Belphégor to give us some little ones. Clotilde was not, it must be said, brimming with enthusiasm at the prospect of a litter of kittens in the apartment. We had never discussed it before, and in any case the vet – no longer the film buff (we had moved to a different arrondissement) – had remarked with surprise that she showed no sign of coming into heat. I got in touch with other cat-owners to arrange dates. The album *One Summer Night* suffered as a result. I spent more time on the telephone discussing feline reproductive issues than I did writing lyrics. I received a furious email from the production company, which I have treasured ever since:

'You'll get your money when the hell ever your cat gets laid…'

Typically, the date nights culminated in atrocious yowling – not Belphégor, but her would-be sex partners, who retreated in terror behind their favourite sofa or their owner's legs. Belphégor categorically refused their advances and any form of sexual intercourse, transforming herself into a bristling ball, like a puffed-up sunfish, before being returned to her carry bag.

'It's you.'

'What do you mean, me?'

'It's you,' the vet insisted. 'She's invested all her affection, all her emotional energy, in you. You saved her from certain death in Parc Montsouris, and now it's you she loves. She thinks of herself as your spouse.'

I stared at him in horror. Belphégor sat majestically on his consulting table.

'Don't look at me like that. Psychology isn't only for humans, you know. They have pet shrinks in the States;

granted, that's taking things a little too far, but the principle is not entirely unfounded. You must have heard those stories about cats who lie down to die on their master's tomb, or who go on a five-hundred-kilometre journey to find them when they've moved. You know all about that, Monsieur Véga.'

Of course I knew all about that. And I hugged Belphégor – my cat-wife – close, with tears in my eyes. The vet's eyes looked a little red, too.

'I had to say goodbye to Armand the day before yesterday,' he said, by way of explanation. 'A Persian,' he added.

'I'm so sorry.'

'Thank you,' he said in a broken voice.

On the evening of the aforementioned consultation with the asthma specialist, my wife asked if we could talk. She asked while we were eating supper, and her tone made it sound like an inquisition, like some big secret that Bruno mustn't understand. We were in the sitting room, nursing glasses of vodka and lime while Bruno did his homework in his room, when my wife stepped gently, cautiously into the forbidden territory.

We would have to let Belphégor go.

Let her go.

Lyricist that I am, those three words cut me like a razor. The conversation that followed went roughly like this:

'You could just give her away.'

'Who to?'

'I don't know… Alain?'

'Alain already has two cats.'

'Well exactly.'

'No, that's impossible. Alain's two cats would never accept a newcomer. It would be dreadful for Belphégor, too.'

'Otherwise…'

'Otherwise what?'

'I'm not… If you don't want to give her away, there's only one other solution.'

I stared at her in horror.

'How could you ask me any such thing?'

'Well, plenty of people would do it…' she said, as naturally as you please. 'We can't let our little baby boy cough like that all the time.'

I said nothing, so she went on:

'I know it upsets you, but—'

'But what?' I said, my voice broken.

This was the moment Belphégor chose to make her entrance and rub herself against my ankles, purring deeply.

'I know she's your cat, and you're very fond of her…' Clotilde continued, 'but the time will come when she's no longer with us anyway… And we're… well, we're here. I'm here, with Bruno, and we're more important. We're your family, not that cat.'

Belphégor walked away – she was probably hoping for a plate of crunchy treats. My wife and I stayed silent, in the sitting room. Belphégor came back again.

'Listen,' said my wife gently. 'There's a choice to be made. You can stay with her, or you can stay with us.' Then she concluded quietly, to herself, 'This is absurd…'

I stared at Belphégor. I gazed deep into the golden pools of her eyes, and I told her:

'I'm staying with you.'

I grappled with the decision for two entire weeks. Two hideous weeks during which I calculated the upheaval that would tear my life apart. I tried to distract myself by watching TV or leafing through magazines. *French Homes*, in particular – one of Clotilde's favourites. The finest residences in France, the most stunning Parisian apartments, were showcased in its pages.

Two weeks went by. Bruno was still coughing. One evening I told Clotilde that I had reached a decision. That I would do it the next day.

'I'll miss her too... I'll tell Bruno we gave her away, and that she's in a house with lots of other cats, and she's happy. That's the best way, for him, don't you think?'

I lay awake all night. Now it was daybreak. Time to say goodbye. I left a note for Clotilde and got Belphégor into her carry bag, with considerable difficulty. Yesterday evening, my wife had wished me strength for the expedition to the vet in the morning. She was quite right. Strength was what I needed for this act of renunciation. Everything seemed perfectly normal, and yet, from that morning on, nothing in my life would be the same again.

I descended the staircase with my beloved Belphégor twisting about in her bag. In the car, I placed her securely on the seat next to me. I poked a finger through the grille on the bag and felt her lustrous fur; an affectionate nibble of her teeth.

I started the engine.

There was really nothing else to be done, I told myself.

In the sitting room, I let my cat out of the bag. She made her way around slowly, then jumped onto a sofa and sharpened her claws voluptuously. This new apartment was ours now. The place where we would live together, just the two of us. She and I.

'How could I possibly have done that to you, my love? My darling cat…' I said, rubbing my face in her fur.

'Of course I'll stay here with you, madame.'

How very formal of me, I hear you say. But this you should know – lyricists have their eccentricities, too. Not just divas and impresarios. I have always addressed Belphégor as 'madame'.

I needed a ten-minute break after Robotti left. The patient had suffered one of his attacks of verbal diarrhoea. The day before yesterday he had thrown his mobile phone out of the window, hoping by this symbolic act of destruction to sever the cord that attached him to his mother, who was in the habit of calling him several times a day on that number. But the telephone had hit a young woman on a moped, who wasn't wearing a crash helmet. Robotti and the woman had gone to the local ambulance station for checks and treatment, and then to the police. They had exchanged numbers and would perhaps see one another again, a prospect which had sunk him deep in an abyss of anxiety.

'I've barely spoken to any woman I don't already know since my divorce,' he said over and over again at the end of the consultation. His divorce was four years ago.

And now, Nathalia. The songwriter, the man with the black cat.

'Do you have a cat?'

'Yes. You're going to ask me if he's black.'

'I'm asking.'

'He's grey. And Vincent's cat is female, not male, if you've read the piece properly.'

'I've read it properly.'

This exchange is unlikely to get us far. I try to open up a more constructive dialogue, because I should like to know if the man with the black cat is an imaginary double, or truly a neighbour in her building? Alice Larjac is real; I've seen her website. Alban is real, without a shadow of a doubt. But I have no way of checking the story she's told me about him – for now. We shouldn't talk about this latest text yet. We should go back to the cartoonist. The comic strip author. Clearly, we are of one mind, because she speaks next, asking the following question:

'Did you go to the book signing?'

I'm going to lie. It's one of my guru Malevinsky's techniques. A way to dust off the dialogue: 'Breathe on the objects under discussion, blow away the dust and their sparkle will be restored. The breath of lies is most effective.'

'No.'

'... is the wrong answer, doctor! I saw you there. I was behind you. You were talking to a blonde woman who likes Voutch and Sempé.'

The breath of lies is proving more effective than I thought. Nathalia was there and I didn't see her. This is more than a slip. This is wilful blindness.

'Why didn't you speak to me?'

'People don't usually meet their shrink outside the consulting room.'

'No indeed. You're approaching your therapy with commendable seriousness, Nathalia.' My tone is – I hope – both authoritative and ironic.

'Thank you, doctor,' she replies, and her tone is identical to my own.

'That said, I thought you never went out?'

She says nothing. I've scored a point. In fact, I may have made my point rather too forcefully – I don't want her to close up tight like an oyster. This has happened to me before, and I dislike it very much. A string of fine phrases that serve nothing but my own stupid pride, and the patient clams up, leaving me to repair the damage. Immediate action is required, in the heat of the moment, or it can take weeks. Worse still, the patient might leave and never return. Nathalia may disappear. I must act quickly to prevent any such thing.

I veer off in a completely different direction. Another of my techniques:

'Share a thought with me that has occurred to you today, completely unrelated to our discussion here. Something absolutely "off topic".'

Silence falls once again, broken only by the beating of a pigeon's wings as it flies past the window.

'I thought… This morning, when I was making coffee… that we should always re-read the epigraph once we've finished a book.'

'Go on.'

'We read a quote from someone other than the author, which the author has chosen to put on the first page of their book, and then we forget all about it. Except the author went to a great deal of trouble to choose it. It sums up the entire book, and then we forget about it. So we should always read it again once the book is finished. Always. The epigraph is the book's true conclusion. That's what I was thinking about.'

I nod. Good. The storm has passed.

'Let's get back to your stories.'

'You want to know if they're true or made up. I thought that wasn't the point. That's what you said when we started out: real or imaginary stories, it doesn't matter.'

'You have a very good memory,' I tell her.

'Yes, I always remember things that interest me.'

'Your last photograph, for example?'

She doesn't reply. I consult my notes. We shall continue. Because I'd like to know. I think she's making them up, and yet there are too many elements drawn from reality, which interfere with the imaginary aspect.

'On the ground floor, you talk about a life coach who works from home, making videos.'

'Alice, or Marie-Edwige…'

'That's her. Next, on the first floor, the topic of weight comes up, and you tell me you struggled with your weight as a teenager.'

'But you know Alban Charvier is real. In fact you've met him.'

'Yes, and Alice Larjac really does have a friend call Aïcha,' I immediately remind her.

Another silence falls. I wait to hear what Nathalia will say next. I know already, word for word:

'I thought you hadn't called her?' The sentence hangs heavy in the air.

I look at her. Normally, she would turn around at this point. It's what my patients tend to do when they catch me out. But she does not turn around.

'You're projecting yourself through these identities. With some talent, indeed. But you are there, in each of these lives.'

She says nothing and I go on:

'What am I to understand from the story of the man who chooses to live with his female cat, rather than with his wife and child?'

'Maybe nothing.'

'What do you mean by that?'

'Take this,' she says, holding up a magazine she's removed from her tote bag. She hands it to me over the back of the couch.

'What is it?'

'You'll see.'

'OK,' I say, and I place the magazine on my desk without a glance. 'Why does he leave?'

'He leaves because his wife has asked him to have Belphégor put to sleep.'

'A monstrous act.'

'She doesn't think of it as monstrous.'

'But it's murder, is that what you're trying to tell me?'

She says nothing.

'Why a lyricist?'

'I like Vincent's songs a lot. They're a little sugary, but we need that. A marshmallow world made of love.'

'Vincent Véga doesn't exist, Nathalia. Neither he nor Belphégor.'

'Why are you so keen for all these people not to exist, doctor?'

Lemont launches into an account of a dream – one he has often, so he says. He's never told me about it before: a tale of butterflies and a boat at low tide. I'm convinced he's making it up as he goes along, just to sound more interesting. I let him get on with his story about a beach and an abandoned boat full of butterflies. Discreetly, I pick up Nathalia's magazine.

Rock & Folk. I find the contents page.

Interview with Vincent Véga, page 54.

On page 54, the photograph shows a man in his forties, his eyes sparkling with intelligence. He's holding a black cat close to his cheek, as if to make sure they're both in the frame. The cat is staring into the camera.

Caption: Vincent Véga with his cat, Belphégor. Photo credit: N.G.

If ever there's a person who's not making everything up as she goes along, it's Nathalia. And so, what if it's true? What if it's all true? What does it all mean, and most importantly, how can what we are doing be classified as therapy? If these are real people's lives, then there's nothing to analyse. Merely facts. And yet I cannot accept the idea. I'm in denial. She is talking to me about herself, and it doesn't matter if Vincent

Véga and his cat Belphégor are real. Or if the life coach has a friend called Aïcha. It doesn't matter if Alban—

'You're not listening, doctor.'

'Oh, I am – you've just told me the butterflies are transparent. Go on.'

'What can my heart possibly be telling you?'

'Quiet please,' says François.

François is a cardiologist. I've known him for thirty years. He's my oldest friend, the one with the dark blue eyes that I had never noticed.

'I'm not happy with this curve,' he says, turning back to his instruments. 'When did you say you stopped smoking?'

'A year ago.'

The corners of François's mouth drop in disbelief as he stares at the graph. He sighs.

'I'm keeping you for a while longer, we'll do an electro, a stress test.'

'I haven't got time.'

'You haven't got time... Well, your neurotics can wait.'

I say nothing, and we go back to his study. I slip my shirt on, and François takes a seat.

'Call me next week. I'll fit you in between two consultations. We should all go out for dinner sometime,' he adds, scribbling notes in my file.

The year has just begun, and I know already that we will utter those words a good half a dozen times before finally fixing a dinner date with our wives. It's like that every year. Neither he nor I are especially keen on the idea, but we will never admit it.

'I'm having a strange recurring dream at the moment,' he says, turning to look at me. 'I'm being stung by a giant bee. Any idea what that means?'

'Buy yourself a dreamcatcher,' I tell him, as I button up my shirt.

'Fuck it, just tell me.'

'It doesn't mean much in my kind of therapy. But others would say it represents a sexual urge, feelings of violent desire.'

'It's Priscilla, I knew it.' I'm staring at him, and he adds: 'A nurse. A new nurse. Twenty-five years old. Huge breasts. My wife has no breasts. It's always frustrated me.'

'François…!' I say, in exaggerated astonishment. And then his phone rings. An internal call. I hear his secretary's voice announcing the name of a well-known presenter whose show is watched nightly by the whole of France.

'I'll be out in a second, Fabienne.'

'Is that the guy off the TV?'

'Yes, he's here for a check-up. He makes time for this sort of thing. People should be more like him.'

I step out into the corridor with François, who introduces me to the television presenter.

'A shrink?' he says, shaking me by the hand. 'Have you published anything?'

'Yes, a few things.'

'Oh really? Anything current?'

'Current?'

'Any books coming out?'

'No.'

'He's lying, he's got a host of books up his sleeve,' François jokes. 'One on erotic dreams, for a start.' He slaps me on the shoulder.

'Is that so?' says the TV host. 'We'd love to get a shrink on the show. Something a bit different. Classy.'

'Dr Faber on the sofa, between a female rapper and a politician!' François is delighted.

'Why ever not? Everyone's ripe for analysis!' The presenter sounds genuinely enthusiastic. 'Do you have a card?'

I stare at him, dumbfounded, and I think about Nathalia's story, in which he's named.

'No, no card. What about you? Do you have a make-up artist by the name of Patricia?'

'Patricia? Absolutely. In fact, I fixed her up with someone just recently. She met Alban, the cartoonist, when he was in make-up, and they've been together ever since. Thanks to who? Thanks to me!' He gestured proudly towards his chest with both hands, fingers outstretched. 'Do you know Patricia?'

'Yes… No… I have to go.'

'So do we! Come on in!' François leads the presenter into his office by the arm. As I walk away, I hear the presenter say:

'You know him personally, you must have his number, his card…'

THIRD FLOOR

To my left, an endless vista of the sea, and waves breaking over the rocks. To my right, the heath. A windswept expanse of long grass and thistles. The contrast is striking, and, so far, I have met no one on the path since the bus dropped me at Pittenweem. I'm in Scotland. My name's Marc Lacour and I never thought that one day I'd be walking all alone on a Scottish heath in search of the Lady's Tower.

I come from a world of computer screens. Flat screens, state of the art, broadband faster than a meteor. The lines I trace are not white, like shooting stars, but coloured, and they shoot up and down like an electrocardiogram – the world's heartbeat. Numbers shoot by, too, at the same speed, top to bottom, in columns. Thousands of numbers per second. Data on the move. Risks being taken – small for some, huge for others. Volume. Markets. Over 7,000 billion dollars change hands around the world every day. And the figure grows constantly, year on year. Like stars that expand and burst. Supernovas. I existed at the heart of the matrix. One among hundreds of thousands of others, scattered around the world. You've got it: I was a trader. A prop trader. Which is to say a proprietary trader: the elite of the banking world, the guys who have carte blanche to speculate on all the capital markets. A high-risk profession, but the rewards are high, too: a percentage of everything you make. Dizzying sums. Dizzying percentages, too. Most traders are very young. But prop traders are the exception: they need the experience. Ten years on the 'floor' is the norm. I was thirty-nine when the 'incident' occurred.

Gusts of wind buffet the heath, and at times I'm almost blown off my feet. With my boots and parka, I'm impervious to the cold, and I find this primeval scene strangely comforting. My hotelier told me that in this part of north-east Scotland you can experience all four seasons in a single day. Right now, I'd say we're approaching the onset of winter. But it was a very different matter this morning. I rose, not at dawn, but just before, when the sky pales to violet before sunrise, at the very end of the night. I walked down a narrow lane beside a field grazed by a dozen or so sheep, until I stood looking out over the bay, where the North Sea and the sky meet to form a great glass dome. I had arrived at the hotel the night before, to a small supper of smoked haddock soup with a glass of rich, peaty whisky. I exchanged a few words with the owner, who mistook me for a French photographer who had left the previous day. He had come to capture the so-called 'fire skies' – this is the best time of year. You had to get up early, said my hotelier, and wait.

I got up early and waited, sitting on a bench marked with a small brass plaque: it had been donated by a Scottish family, in memory of MARGARETH, whose life dates were engraved below her name, together with a few words noting that she had loved to walk here.

From violet, the sky turned to orange streaked with grey. The colours shifted in the blink of an eye, like vivid inks blending on a sheet of wet paper. Orange was the dominant hue now, at its most intense on the horizon, just above the line of the sea. In the distance, a point of light appeared, like the head of a pin: the sun. The orange turned fluorescent, and the streaks of grey turned red. A deep, intense red. The whole sky became red, shot through with orange above the sea, which took on the colours of the sky in turn. The fire sky. I stood up and walked a few paces, slowly, as if trying to step out into the light, to touch it, to become one with it. I took off my gloves. I wanted to take a photograph, but the cold shut down my phone instantly (my battery was at just 10 per cent). I took this as a sign: look with your own eyes, your heart, and remember, you don't need a screen between you and the world. Not any more. Not now.

That was this morning.

I carry on walking, and now a couple are silhouetted in the distance, on the beach. The man is throwing a stick for a dog who chases it and brings it back. The man holds out the stick to the woman, who throws it in her turn. Again, the dog chases after it. A kind of perpetual motion, delightful, beautiful. Human.

In another life, my life as a trader, I never did delightful things like walk a dog on a beach in the company of a woman, throwing a stick for a dog to fetch, over and over. Instead, I bought idiotic contemporary art on the advice of a gallerist, including a Damien Hirst made from butterfly wings, which I ended up loathing. It took pride of place in my sitting room. A few other bits by Jeff Koons. A Ferrari that I drove precisely three times, giving myself such a fright that I sold it to another trader, a braver soul than I in affairs of the motorcar. I bought the most expensive watch brands, including a Richard Mille with so many cogs and complications that I actually found it impossible to tell the time. I had become a kind of living cliché of success in today's consumer society. I travelled, and I partied in fashionable locations, spent time with other guys like me, who wore the same bespoke tailored suits, the same watches, and hung the same pieces of idiotic contemporary art on their walls. The same women... Beautiful, tall, thin, long-legged – wild animals who treated us like prey. Which is what we were. I took fright when I almost got mixed up in cocaine. I saw myself snorting a line at a party, and a voice inside told me that this time I'd gone too far. I looked across at the young woman I was with at the time. She was sniffing it up, laughing with a girlfriend, and I asked myself if I had chosen the right life partner.

'You're no fun, Marc,' she told me a few weeks later before we broke up. She was right. None of this made me laugh now.

I went out less, focused on my work. I sold the Damien Hirst. I lost touch with a fair few of my contacts, who were leaving for London, New York, Dubai. All of them wondered why I chose to stay put in my 'patch', in Paris–La Défense. I was one of the best in the business now, but staying in alone every night. I shut myself away. I lost the keys to life in the real world. After an entire day staring at figures on-screen, I'd spend the evening back at home staring at YouTube videos, to deaden my brain. Some porn, too. I joined Tinder. My meet-ups were all disappointing. We don't need a new metaverse, we're there already – everything takes place in front of a screen. Holiday snaps are stored on Instagram, or the 'Photos' tab on Facebook. Cloud memories. Women you might meet one day are all inside an app or on a website. You just have to send them a message.

'We live more in the life we do not have than in the life we do,' said a poet or writer whose name I've forgotten, long ago. And now, it seems to me that we live more in our online lives than in life itself. Enough philosophy. It's not my strong point, and I'll only bore you. Let me tell you about 'the incident'. Let me tell you why I'm on a Scottish hiking trail that leads to the Lady's Tower.

But before I tell you about the incident, I need to tell you about the Tower. It was the screensaver on my laptop. It still is. When you open up your computer, and before it asks for your password, it will generally show you a picture selected by an algorithm: a landscape, an animal, greenery, a historic monument... A desert dune by moonlight, a view of Dubai from one of its skyscrapers, a panda surrounded by bamboo. Usually, I ignore it and punch in my password; the suggested picture disappears straight away. One day, the screen showed a picture of a round, stone-built tower – rough-cut blocks piled one on top of the other. Neither tall nor small, the tower was entered through an arched opening. It stood on bare heathland overlooking the sea, a partial ruin suffused with a sense of calm and infinite time that prompted me to take a screenshot, save it, and make it my permanent screensaver. But I had neglected to check the information link, and its location. The tower remained a mystery. A mystery that haunted me every time I switched on my computer.

Sometimes, I would find myself gazing at it as if hypnotised; my mind would wander all around the monument, and inside it, before I came to my senses. (Fact: apparently we fall into a hypnotic state roughly ten times a day – for a few seconds only.) Anyway, one Sunday, alone in my apartment, I tapped 'tour', 'landes' and 'mer' into my search engine. A host of images appeared, but none of 'my' tower. An English-language search on '*tower*', '*landscapes*' and '*sea*' produced nothing better. This was becoming an obsession. Where was the tower? In France? Italy? Germany? Was it in England? Or Latin America? What was the ocean, or the sea, all around the headland on which it stood? My fruitless search filled the entire afternoon, drawing me deeper and deeper into the internet; until I found a forum for ancient tower enthusiasts. Seriously, you can find anything online. I signed up and, once I'd been accepted as a member, I was able to post my photograph of the tower and ask, in several languages, whether anyone recognised it.

★

A few days later I received a message in English from a member of the group. I don't remember his pseudonym, but his message read:

'Hi. Yes, I know where this is – it's the Lady's Tower in Elie, Scotland.' I immediately typed the name into my search engine straight away and found more pictures of my tower, together with an explanation of its curious name. I'll tell you about that later.

Now I'm passing by a tall mill on the edge of St Monans, a fishing village with a harbour and a church that overlooks the sea. I pause to buy a small bottle of water – walking in the wind makes you thirsty. In front of the church, the cemetery's dishevelled tombstones look as if they've been here since the dawn of time. I check my GPS; I'm on the right trail; I'm almost there. Keep to the coast path all the way along. I find a route right beside the water, before climbing up to the heathland once again. The sea is quite rough. I am showered with spray.

And now, the incident: one year ago. I was on the twenty-eighth floor of our tower in La Défense, in a vast, open-plan trading office, seated in front of my screens like everyone else – roughly six screens per trader. I was lounging in my office chair, playing for high stakes; very high stakes, just as I had for the past few months or more. I'll spare you a detailed description of my investment strategy and portfolio – there's only one other trader on the planet who'd understand it. But in essence, I was betting on a decline in volume followed by an upturn that would allow me to sell the stash I had accumulated over the past few months at a more than substantial profit. My stash had grown that very afternoon and now stood at... a billion dollars. The anticipated fall was connected to the announcement of a massive stock acquisition by a group initially hailed as a complete outsider. I had the information, the informers, everything. The news broke at 2.15 p.m. French time. I had the right information, the right hunch. My plan was working perfectly. The biggest coup of my career. Except for... the share price. Instead of falling then recovering, it began to rise. Straight up, like an arrow, soaring from one minute to the next. After twenty-five minutes, I'd accumulated losses of 800 million euros. I stared at my screens, open-mouthed. And on it went. A billion euros now. At that instant, I had taken the bank and its investors for a billion euros, then 1.1 billion, and rising... I turned ice-cold. Rivulets of scalding sweat trickled over my temples. The names of every famous trader who had lost colossal sums over the past forty years buzzed around me like a swarm of wasps. Toshihide Iguchi in the 1980s: 1.1 billion dollars. And since then, Nick Leeson: 1.3 billion. Brian Hunter, in 2006: 6.5 billion. Jérôme Kerviel, just two years before: 4.9 billion. And still the losses were mounting. It was out of my control. The screens blurred before my eyes. I blinked and tried to refocus on the columns, gasping for air all the while. The share price was still rising. And the higher it rose, the more I lost.

'What the fuck...?' I whispered under my breath.

At almost 2 billion dollars, my hands began to shake, and I found it hard to swallow. I gave it one last shot, all or nothing – and again this would be too complicated to explain, but I took the only way out, the only option left to me. I could try to recover everything or quadruple my losses and break even Jérôme Kerviel's record by losing 8 billion dollars outright. I took everything back and placed it on crypto instead. The newest bad boy on the block. The financial markets are a madhouse run by madmen. I truly believe the lunatics have taken over the asylum. I know this for a fact because I almost went insane. My extreme positions provoked a mini tsunami in the lines on my screens: where had these crazy amounts come from, invested all at once? The market took fright. I was busy now, turning the share price's upward-shooting arrow back around and down. I had caused panic in the markets, but the wildly fluctuating lines were nothing as compared to my own heartbeat. I had just a few minutes to play the wildest wild card of my life, then wait for the price to fall to my desired level before pulling suddenly out of crypto and placing everything back where it had started. Profits: zero. Losses: zero. Twelve minutes from start to finish. On my personal laptop screen, Bloomberg TV reported an inexplicable, record investment in crypto, with no clue where it had come from. If they only knew... The longest twelve minutes of my life. My mouth was bone dry. Take back 2 billion and place it elsewhere. Quick, quick... The curves were sinking. Now... I pulled everything out and placed it one more time. My curves shifted gently, gently, then stabilised at 1 billion. That was when I stopped trading. Left the market. Losses: zero. Gains: zero. I was struggling to breathe. I stared at the screens. Losses: zero. Gains: zero. 'I've done it,' I whispered, but no sound came out of my mouth. I turned to look at the breaking news from Bloomberg TV: the picture disappeared, and my screensaver of the Lady's Tower took its place. Then I felt every muscle in my body go limp. I sank back into the soft leather of my office chair. And at that moment I saw myself. Me. I was floating, looking down at my inert body as it stared, wide-eyed, at the screenshot of the Scottish tower. Then I slumped to the floor and my colleagues surrounded me. I was floating, weightless above the open-plan trading floor. I could see everything. I knew I was dead. Probably from cardiac arrest. But the thought washed over me as a simple statement of fact. I wasn't the least bit concerned. On the contrary, with each passing second, I felt happier, lighter, I was floating above the trading floor, and then I floated out through the great plate-glass window, and carried on floating outside, above the great parvis of La Défense, with its arch and its skyscrapers. I looked up at the sky and was filled with a sense of infinite well-being, when a hole opened in the clouds – a strange weather phenomenon I had never seen before. It was calling me in. Finally, I entered a corridor of light, unnaturally bright, though it did not hurt my eyes. I knew there were others around me, but I could not see them. I felt their presence. Then the light became brighter still, until it pervaded everything with an intensity and harmony that is not of this world. I felt happier than I had ever felt before. Everything was so simple. Here was everything, and nothing, all at once. As if a great, classical symphony was ringing out, while silence reigned. I was in a state of pure joy. *No. Now is not the time.* No one had spoken these words. There was no voice to be heard. Nothing had been stated in the ways we know here below. No specific language had been used. This was of another order entirely. A statement of fact, and at the same time very much an order. Things became somehow inverted, and I felt myself returning to the place from which I had come.

I opened my eyes in a speeding ambulance with its siren wailing. The hospital kept me in for five days of tests and observation. I was a curious case, according to the doctor in charge of my care. I showed no signs of having suffered a heart attack. The extensive battery of tests to which I had been subjected had revealed nothing at all. And yet, he said, I had died. Not on the trading floor but in the ambulance, for four minutes, before I woke up.

'You were clinically dead,' he told me, 'and then you came back.' He added that I had suffered no ill effects. I had undergone an NDE – a near-death experience. He paused for a moment and looked at me. My face was calm, and I was smiling serenely. Then he asked a question:

'Did you see anything?'

I shook my head slowly from left to right, meaning to say that I had seen nothing at all. It was as if the force that had brought me back from the light to my own body had asked me to keep the experience to myself. And so I did.

I had been given to understand the meaning of life, and mine would not now be spent in front of a bank of screens, tracking the pulse of this mad, mad world from one billion-dollar deal to the next. I resigned my post and was roundly condemned for failing to take a position on an incredible deal that had earned hundreds of millions for others in the business. My employers would never know the catastrophe they had been spared. I sold all my watches, my objets d'art and my contemporary paintings. I sold everything in my apartment until all that remained was a bed, a sofa and a desk. I knew what I must do, as a kind of rite of passage… I had to visit the last thing I had seen in my former life: the Lady's Tower, my screensaver. I booked a flight to Scotland, and the requisite train and bus tickets. I took a room in a hotel. On the appointed date, an Airbus A320 took off from Roissy-Charles-de-Gaulle, bound for Edinburgh.

I can just about see it now, away in the distance, on a tongue of land that reaches out into the sea beside the waters of Ruby Bay, named for the semi-precious stones – red garnets, not rubies – which are found embedded in its volcanic rock. It forms a small rectangle, silhouetted against the light, standing out against an increasingly blue sky, swept by a sea breeze that's chasing the clouds inland. I walk on. I'm getting closer. The Lady's Tower is named for Lady Janet Anstruther, the daughter of a merchant in the nearby village of Elie, renowned for her bewitching beauty, such that the local gossips whispered she was born of gypsy blood. She had silenced her naysayers by marrying the local laird, Sir John Anstruther, who had fallen madly in love with her. Janet's portrait was painted by Sir Joshua Reynolds, and is now in the collection of the Tate Gallery, in London. Janet loved to swim in the summer months, and in 1770 she had the tower built for her private use. She also arranged for a cave to be dug in the rock nearby, open to the beach, so that she could undress and bathe... in the nude! After parting the waters of the salty North Sea with her languorous breaststroke, she would emerge naked as Eve and retreat to her tower to gaze at the sea and sky while she dried in the warm sun. A bell was set up nearby, to be rung by a servant just before Lady Janet took her beauty dip. No one in Elie was allowed to approach the shore or even look in its direction while she swam. Her servants would turn their backs and stare fixedly inland. The bell was only rung again once Lady Janet had slipped into her bathrobe. Life could resume. And no one, apart from Sir John, ever saw Lady Janet naked. Except perhaps a few mischievous children hiding among the thistles. But on that, the record is silent.

A footpath leads in a straight line, right up to the entrance. I reach the tower and gaze up at it. Two benches face one another, on either side. I step inside and find myself standing in the middle of a circle. There are several arches, in fact, but you cannot tell this from the photographs. Through each opening, there is a view of the sea. The sky is bright blue, as if it had suddenly become summer. I am here. I am inside the Lady's Tower, my screensaver. I reach out and touch the stone, just to be sure it's real. Then I gaze out to sea, to infinity, lulled by the soft sigh of the retreating waves and the breeze that whistles through the chinks in the walls. A white sail passes in the distance, on the horizon. Slowly, I turn around on the spot. I can't believe I'm here. I feel happy and carefree.

I go down to the beach and find the shadowy cave, carved from the living rock, hard as iron. This is where Lady Janet would disrobe before stepping out naked into the wavelets. The beach where she bathed is a small, sandy bay dotted with red and ochre rocks, some almost perfectly rounded, giving this section of coastline the look of a landscape from science fiction – like the surface of Mars, but lapped by the sea.

I walk back up to the tower, to find one of the benches occupied now by a young woman reading a book, basking in the sunshine while the breeze plays with her long, dark hair. She's wearing glasses and a beige-coloured coat. I sit down on the opposite bench, a few metres away. For a minute or more, nothing happens. She is absorbed in her book, and I, in the landscape all around. Then she looks up and our eyes meet. I smile. I squint to read the title on the cover of her novel, and she holds it up in front of her face, so that I can see it.

Soon, we are chatting about the book, because I read it myself a few years ago. Then we find ourselves in an almost deserted pub, sitting beside the glowing embers of a fire, conversing in English about France and Scotland, and my French accent, and the Lady's Tower. She's delighted by my tale of stepping inside my own screensaver. She nods gravely when I tell her what I used to do for a living, and that I have left my job. Her name is Mary. She works in a pottery in the next village. She makes vases, cups, plates. I look at her hands that shape the wet clay on a potter's wheel. She tells me she's been here for two years. At no point does she mention a husband or partner. She invites me to come and watch her at work, and I think that the light I saw may have brought Mary

121

to me, so that I would not regret turning back to the land of the living. I'll watch her as she works, and just then she will turn her face to the sunlit window pane, and I will ask myself if she is the appointment I was meant to keep in this place.

The appointment I was meant to keep all along.

But no.

In truth, I shall ask myself no such question.

I already know the answer.

Since the beginning of the afternoon, I've had nothing to do but wait for Nathalia. I had slotted in Lemont and Robotti – my two Oedipal complexes – one after the other. I'd placed them in that order for the very first time, a decision judged inacceptable, it seems, by some malevolent spirit, because the two of them failed to turn up for their sessions.

Both together, as if by prior arrangement. The twin complex personified. Perhaps they really had acted in concertation with one another? Patients never meet in the waiting room, but I have no idea what happens in the world beyond, on the staircase, in the hallway, or the café where they wait – perhaps – for their appointment. After all, Madame Garcia, the picture restorer (melancholic depression), found a life partner in Monsieur Champerrois (manic obsessive-compulsive disorder). He never went out without gloves and washed his hands twenty times a day. Both of them had quit their analysis abruptly, taking it in turns to announce their new-found love and the end of their respective troubles. I never knew how the two of them met.

'Thank you for the hike across the Scottish heath – most invigorating,' I tell her.

'My pleasure,' she replies, smiling, her eyes fixed firmly on the wall.

Of course, I had checked that the Lady's Tower existed, as I was sure it did: the pictures on my screen matched the tower in Nathalia's narrative down to the last detail.

'I suppose you've already been to the east coast of Scotland and set foot inside the tower?'

'Never. I might go one day. Perhaps.'

Was she lying? Perhaps not... How to tell?

'And yet, reading your description, I feel as if I am there.'

'Thank you,' she answers politely, adding, 'It shows I'm making progress with my writing.'

For a moment, I feel like a publisher in discussion with a first-time author. At least, I imagine this is the sort of conversation they might have. We need to resume our respective roles: therapist and patient.

'A man who steps inside his screensaver, into an image, so that he can bring it to life. And in that same image, he finds a woman who appears to him as a promise of true love, at last.'

'You summarise it beautifully,' she says. Her voice is measured, calm.

I do not say thank you, but continue:

'On the one hand, a picture; on the other, life. Your narrative abolishes the boundary between the two. It's your job to take pictures.'

She is silent for a moment. Then:

'He asked me to photograph him in his apartment. He was

planning to sell everything. He said: "I want just one souvenir of my past life and who I was before." In my photograph, he's sitting on his sofa. I asked him to rest his hands on his knees and look straight ahead at the camera, at me. I wanted the picture to have a David Hockney-esque feel. Have you seen Hockney's portraits? They all have that slightly awkward, static quality.'

I nod. I can picture Hockney's paintings – I went to an exhibition of his at the Centre Pompidou with my wife. And I've seen his work in museums.

'I asked him where he wanted to go,' she went on. 'He said: "Very far away." Then he smiled and told me: "But first, there's a place I want to visit." He didn't say anything else about that, and I didn't insist. I took my photograph. "I'll be in touch," he said when I presented him with the print. He paid in cash, just like I do here, with you. And he kept his word: he did get in touch, not long ago.'

'How did he know you were a photographer?'

'He saw me taking pictures in the courtyard of our building: I photograph the tree in all seasons. We chatted that day.'

She says nothing more. I don't insist. I go back to my first idea:

'He steps inside a picture, sees it for real, and finds freedom.'

'He finds freedom before that,' Nathalia points out. 'He makes a choice, a change of life. He takes a decision.'

'What about you, Nathalia, what choice have you made?'

'I've chosen to come and see you.'

★

'The session's over,' I tell her. She leaves her money on the desk and with it, as usual, a clue.

'Here,' she says, and she hands me a business card printed with a photograph of a cottage. 'This is their house, their address. They do bed-and-breakfast, if ever you feel like a trip to Scotland. It looks lovely.'

'Wait – who's living in his apartment now?'

'No one,' she says. 'The shutters have been closed for months. He hasn't put it up for sale. I think he can afford to keep it.'

Nathalia has left. I open the website for Thistle Cottage. A couple stands smiling in the doorway. Mary and Marc, with a short biography for each of them, behind the tab marked 'About Us'. She really is a potter; she's Scottish, he's French. He had a career in international finance before choosing a 'new life'. He has given money for the restoration of several lighthouses in the region. Nothing at all about the near-death experience, nor where they met. But two things strike me: first, the village is very close to the Lady's Tower, and second, Marc Lacour is real – I'm looking at his photograph on my screen. A man with a broad, serene, open smile. Perhaps everyone who has crossed to the other side, and seen the tunnel and the light, wears that same smile. What do they know that we do not?

This morning, I woke at dawn and watched as the first pale light of day filtered into the silent apartment through the yellow curtains. A curious effect, like warm sunshine. And I told myself it was summer; I was able to convince myself of this quite easily, and it comforted me.

Like my patients, I'm affected by the weather, and so I kept the curtains closed. I had no desire to see the grey skies and rain outside. I went into my daughter's old room, which my wife has requisitioned now as an extension of her office at work, a place to store documents connected to her journalism for the paper. Catherine's CDs are stacked in a small pile on the shelf, with a few books and an empty cigarette packet, signed by a singer she once worshipped, whose writing I can't read. It had been her most treasured possession, but it lies forgotten now.

I found myself pondering how we fetishise objects, and magical thinking, and I remembered texts I had read about these in the past. But it was very early and I took it no further. I looked at the CD jackets. The singers' names meant nothing to me, but one image caught my eye: against a turquoise backdrop that looks as if it's been painted roughly with a roller, a man in a purple shirt sits astride a chair turned the wrong way around, resting his forehead on one hand, as if he's reached the end of the line. Alain Bashung.

I slot the disc – itself coloured bright turquoise – into the player, with the volume down low because my wife is still asleep. I skim through the tracks at random. A clean, metallic sound fills the room, with a quasi-religious feel, and then Bashung's bitter, disenchanted voice intones strange-sounding words, something about a beekeeper, and oaths, and certainties.

Catherine loved this song. She would listen to it over and over again. I remember the haunting melody, the sermon-like quality, the voice that seemed to speak from deep inside a church, imploring the angels, or young girls. And then the last lines – an oasis, and an avenue lined with docile spaniels.

My dream from the other night. The words of a singer I'd long since forgotten. The brain really is an uncharted continent. It's all there, I told myself, tucked away between chance or fate and the work of therapy. And another emotion crept over me, an overwhelming feeling of affection. A feeling to which I could put a name.

A young woman's name: Nathalia. Sitting there in my daughter's old room, what I felt was not romantic love. This was stronger altogether: I wished that Nathalia could have been my daughter.

There's something of me in her, I told myself.

Now my wife and I are having breakfast together. Coffee with milk for her, in a cup. Black coffee for me, in a bowl.

I open the brown paper envelope. It contains eight sheets of blank white paper, stapled together. I flip through them, turning each one back with my thumb and index finger.

'Has your patient run out of inspiration?'

'I don't know… Perhaps she wants to stop,' I say, and my irritation is plain to hear.

'That's a shame, she was good.'

'I'm sorry?'

'She was good. Her writing. Her stories…' she says, pouring milk.

'You read them?' I stare at her in astonishment.

'She never sealed the envelopes. They were very entertaining.'

'Entertaining? They were set as an exercise in a therapeutic context.'

'I wasn't breaking her confidentiality as a patient, they were just stories,' she says off-handedly.

'Stories in which she talks about herself. It's private,' I remind her.

'Does it really bother you that I've read them?' She stirs her milky coffee.

'Yes, it does.' I crush a stubborn sugar cube at the bottom of my bowl. 'I'm perfectly happy to tell you about them, but you shouldn't have read them yourself.'

'Why ever not? You read the paper, and I'm responsible for a great many things you see in—'

'That's different. These pieces were written for me. For me alone.'

We sit in silence. I stir my bowl of coffee, in which the sugar seems determined not to dissolve this morning.

'And according to you alone, why are the sheets of paper all blank this time?' My wife's voice is heavy with irony.

'She hasn't found a new story through which to present herself. Or she wants to stop.'

'So you won't see her again... Stop rattling that spoon, you'll break the bowl.'

'The sugar won't dissolve.'

She rolls her eyes to the ceiling in mock anguish. Then she looks at me across the table.

'You're annoyed.'

I make no reply.

'You valued that patient.'

'Yes, I value all my patients.'

'Not all of them are blessed with her imagination,' she says. 'Oh, and is she pretty, too?'

I want to say yes, she's pretty, very pretty – other girls are dull and ugly compared with Nathalia. But my wife would ask too many questions, and I don't want to talk to her now. People pay to talk to me, after all.

'I know why the pages are blank,' she says.

'Go on, I'm listening…'

'Do you speak to them in that tone of voice…? Your poor patients. I bet they hardly say a word.'

I close my eyes and channel Malevinsky's intonation as I speak the ritual opening words:

'What are you thinking?'

'I'm thinking… that there's no one on the fourth floor.'

'There's no one on the fourth floor.'

'Bravo, doctor.' She claps her hands slowly, three times.

For once, my wife surprises me. It is she who handed me the ice-pick for my continued ascent of the north wing, the black icefield of the subconscious, but I am careful not to let Nathalia know that the idea did not come from me. My wife must not come between us.

'And why is no one there?'

'It's to do with a court case between members of the same family,' she tells me. 'The old lady died five years ago and didn't make a will. There are seals on the doors.'

'You could have told me about her. You told me all about the trader, and he doesn't live in your building any more.'

'I wasn't there five years ago. I've only known this apartment empty.'

I close my eyes and take a deep breath. In the silence of the office, this will add weight to what I am about to say next. It's a phenomenon I've observed before. It's a thing I do when the patient is a little too sure of themselves, when they forget that they are on the couch and that whatever they say is of value to me. And to them, though they often fail to realise that.

'I'm going to tell you what I think. I think you believe you've told me everything about yourself. That's why you've stopped.'

'Do you want me to stop?'

My turn to say nothing in reply.

The silence in the room is overlaid by something I have felt before on several occasions: that sense of the uncanny. Freud. The term comes to mind now, as well as my talks with Malevinsky. I was roughly the same age as Nathalia, and he was my teacher. He seemed very old to me at the time; I was a young disciple, very taken with psychoanalysis, and I followed his classes with a passion. Little by little, we grew to like one another, until he suggested I come to his home for coffee, on Quai de la Mégisserie overlooking the Île de la Cité, in the heart of Paris. To reach the door of his building I had to walk past the market stallholders selling pets and houseplants that line the street along this stretch of the Right Bank of the Seine. Malevinsky liked to settle himself comfortably in an armchair and lose himself in odd thoughts which he would communicate in short, enigmatic phrases. On the day in question, we were discussing a specific topic in analysis: the uncanny, defined by Freud as a sense of disquieting strangeness, but reconfigured by Malevinsky as 'uncertain, or hesitant, certainty'. I asked him what he meant by this, and as usual, he took a roundabout route in reply:

'You walked past the bird-seller downstairs?'

'Yes.'

'Did you see the young blue-and-yellow parrot in the small cage next to the palm trees?'

'No, I didn't notice it.'

'Take a look at it when you leave. It hatched two weeks ago.'

Silence fell, broken by me, with a tentative:

'And so?'

'And so, parrots can live for a hundred years.'

I said nothing, and so he continued:

'Have you considered, young man, that this creature will outlive us? Decades after my death and yours, that bird will still be here.'

Still I said nothing, and so he went on:

'And one feels a very particular sensation, thinking about that.'

'Yes,' I said. 'A sense of strangeness. The uncanny…'

'Or perhaps…?'

'A certainty that we find hard to accept? An uncertain, or hesitant, certainty.'

A year went by, and when spring came I visited the flower market to buy some orchids, which my wife likes to put out in pots on the balcony. My footsteps led me to Quai de la Mégisserie and the big blue door of the building where Malevinsky once lived. I had avoided coming here since his death – I was too upset, nostalgic for our conversations and the knowledge he would drip-feed, in his mischievous, world-weary way.

I looked through the bird-seller's window, and there, near the counter, perched on some sort of coat-stand, I saw a blue-and-yellow parrot. A large, adult bird that seemed to return my gaze. He folded his beady eye into the wrinkled, rubbery skin of his eyelid, and turned his head. It was him – the bird that would outlive me.

I feel the urge to abandon our therapeutic work and hold a proper conversation with her, to ask her why she's here, on my couch, and the meaning of her stories, never entirely real nor entirely made-up. Now I think of it, the idea of the stories for every floor of the building came from her. When she told me she kept a diary and observed her neighbours, I was left with little choice but to ask her to write their stories for me. She spoke so little that writing had seemed the only way to communicate. The idea was hers, not mine. It had all come from her, right from the start.

'Nathalia?'

'Doctor?'

'You are not suffering from depression.'

She says nothing, and I take her silence as an admission.

'You are searching for something, there's a mystical form to your quest.'

'Well observed, doctor.'

'Every mystical form has its journey, its obstacles. You transform with each new test, by changing your identity.'

'And yet these people are real.'

'Yes. Is it important for them to exist in reality?'

'Yes.'

'Why?'

'For the whole.'

'What whole?'

'The whole of the north wing. As an ensemble.'

'But there are only five floors. Or so you told me.'

'Yes.'

'We've come to the end.'

'Yes.'

'Who is on the fifth floor?'

'Mademoiselle Hitahido.'

'Who is she?'

'A Japanese lady. She only comes twice a year, for two weeks in autumn and in the summer.'

'That's not what your story will be about.'

'How do you know?'

'So far, you've never announced the character on the next floor before delivering your piece.'

'True. She won't be my next story.'

'What have you seen, Nathalia?'

'You'll find out, doctor.'

I settle into my armchair and rub my hands slowly over my face. When I look up, my diary is lying open with the list of this afternoon's patients spread out across the page. Four to go. Including Robotti, who has taken a new appointment. He owes me for his last two sessions. I work out how much and note it down next to his name. With Nathalia gone, it feels as if my working day is done.

I shall say nothing at all to Robotti, for the whole of his session. That'll teach him.

My wife has already left when I get up. The breakfast table is laid. I don't understand why she didn't wake me up. As a rule, she gets up at 7 to get to the paper at 9.

Her alarm always rings at 7 a.m., mine at 8. She always sets the table and then comes to wake me at about 7.30, so that we can take breakfast together.

When my alarm sounds, half an hour later, it signals the end of breakfast and our reading of the morning papers. That's how things have been for the past twenty-four years. Twenty-four years of me getting up half an hour too soon. If you take five working days per week, my wife has deprived me of 6,240 half-hours of sleep. Or 3,120 hours. Roughly 130 days, which is to say four-and-a-half months of sleep. Eleven million, two hundred and thirty-two thousand seconds of slumber, and for the first time, I feel as if I'm late when in fact, at last, I'm on time.

The brown paper envelope has been placed where I sit. My wife has opened it and read its contents. That must be why she forgot to wake me up. It irritates me that she read it, and at the same time it touches me to see that she has carefully tucked the flap back inside, as if nothing has happened. For my part, I'll only read it half an hour before Nathalia arrives for her session. Fifteen minutes' reading time, fifteen minutes to reflect on what she has written, then she'll arrive, and we'll talk about it.

FIFTH FLOOR

I am Marco di Caro's last patient.

From now on, I will smoke once a year on the twelfth of March, at 4 p.m. precisely.

Anyone who knew me before would have seen another man altogether. A smoker, complete with that integral part of his body, a cigarette.

Forever wedged between my forefinger and my index finger, my Gauloise Blonde was with me from breakfast through to bedtime. My loyal companion since the age of fifteen, when I bought my first-ever packet of cigarettes in secret, unbeknown to my parents, from a tobacconist near Place du Châtelet.

'A packet of Gauloises and a box of matches, please.'

The tobacconist took my money and held out the small, sky-blue rectangle. The brand I would smoke for the next four years.

I remember that it was very windy that day: I had to shelter behind the panels of a building site near the Pont-Neuf in order to light my first Gauloise, which I did on the eighth attempt. There were specks of tobacco on my tongue. The wind made the tip glow, and the blue smoke was swept away on the air instantly. An inconclusive experience. I hadn't yet worked out how to inhale the smoke, so I blew it out through my nostrils and felt that this delicate operation, completed without coughing, was already something of an exploit.

Months passed and I became expert in the lighting and smoking of filterless Gauloises Brunes. No more cigarette ends disintegrating in the saliva on my lips, no more bitter-tasting specks of tobacco crunched between my teeth. I could even smoke a cigarette held fast between my lips. This operation seems simple enough to non-smokers or hardened smokers who have forgotten their first steps in the art, but to enjoy your cigarette 'hands-free', such that the thin line of smoke rising from the tip does not get in your eyes, is a skill granted to few without extensive practice. If, on the other hand, you smoke hands-free, and the occasional blue-tinted whorl of smoke comes to die betwixt eyeball and lid, you will give a fine demonstration of weeping copiously from one eye, then rubbing it, holding it open to the air, wincing... In short, you will look ridiculous. The feeling – and here, I address the non-smokers in particular – is similar to that when a trickle of shampoo foam insinuates its way surreptitiously onto the surface of your eye.

You thrash about in your bath like a beached carp, cursing and swearing, you prise open your eye to bathe it in copious lashings of clean water. In short, you look ridiculous.

But unlike a bar, a restaurant or a café terrace, no one can see you in your tub. Smoking demands to be done well. And I was a gifted smoker. A very gifted smoker.

After four years of Gauloises, I began to take my pleasure elsewhere. As in a relationship, when one tires of one's partner too quickly, I set out to conquer other blondes, other brunettes. The Gitanes packet, immortalised by Serge Gainsbourg, took the place of my Gauloises for ever. I made it mine – it was more stylish, more practical, except when the last two left in the pack fought a bitter duel and emerged from my trouser pocket limp and crushed.

Next came a broad spectrum of blondes, all of them British: Benson & Hedges, Dunhill Reds (my favourites), Craven A, one of the finest cigarette packets the world has ever known, with its bright red background and its black cat's head, elegant as a bottle of spirits. Sobranies were the chicest blondes, without question, styled for the ladies, with their gold filters and coloured papers: green, blue, yellow, mauve. Very chic, designed to be seen, and kept for special occasions. The gentleman's model, if I may call it that, is black. The filter tip is still gold, but the cigarette paper is a deep matt black, as if dipped in Indian ink.

After that, came extensive trials involving different levels of nicotine and tar: lights, super-lights, ultra-lights, extras, specials...

Cigarettes entered my life like a lover. Like the sort of woman you see on any street corner, selling herself for your spare cash, a woman who's always available, a woman you convince yourself will be faithful to you alone, a woman who will never leave. Unless you decide to throw her out suddenly, one day, whereupon she leaves a void in your heart, in your lungs, so great that you hurry to take her back. Willingly she returns. No pleading or wheedling required. I was in love with my cigarettes. A day without them was inconceivable. From time to time, on the advice of the other love of my life – my wife – I would try to end the affair. But my bigamous existence was so entrenched that my attempts to break it off invariably left me in the foulest of moods, provoking a near-nervous breakdown on my wife's part, and the hasty purchase of a packet of blondes at the bistro on the corner. It was impossible. Try as I might – and try I most certainly did, again and again – each failed attempt, each tender reunion, brought a special joy of its own. Whenever we left for the country, I would convince myself I could stop smoking. I would leave my packets and lighters – my Dunhill, Dupont, Cartier, Zippo – in Paris.

Another brief digression for the non-smokers. Is it not, dear friends, you who detest us the most, a sweet delight to have a husband, mistress, friend, brother or sister who smokes, when Christmas, or their birthday, comes around? You know already what will give us the greatest pleasure – a smart new lighter, a beautiful ashtray, a rare, imported packet, a luxury cigar, and voilà! You never need to rack your brains, never need to ask 'What would he like?' You know perfectly well, and you like it that way – admit it.

★

Back to my weekends in the fresh country air.

Invariably, after 300 kilometres without a cigarette, I was seriously on edge. My wife would heave a sigh of resignation.

'Go on, light up.'

'I didn't bring any with me.'

'Brilliant.'

We would arrive around noon. After lunch, my craving would be worse still. My tiny porcelain coffee cup was crying out for its long, tall, pale, smoky companion. By 4 p.m. the situation would be untenable. By 6, I was bordering on insanity. Stalking the orchard, I would stare wildly around for a cigarette tree. At 8 p.m., barely sentient, I would disappear five minutes before dinner, ready to drive 70 kilometres to the nearest tabac. One New Year's weekend, I actually drove a 130-kilometre round trip.

It was in this state, one year, that we set out with friends for a night at the theatre. After two hours of a thoroughly incomprehensible performance during which I tried and failed several times to fall asleep, we ate dinner on the terrace of a charming brasserie.

'Cigarette, Pascal?' I offered.

'No… I've quit.'

'Really? You'll be back,' I smiled.

'I doubt that very much,' he said confidently.

'And why is that?'

'You've heard of hypnosis for smokers?'

I grinned as I lit one of my faithful companions.

'Don't laugh,' said Michel. He was quite right. In the weeks that followed, I didn't laugh at all. Not once.

Back at home, my wife and I embraced tenderly on the bed. Once again I struggled with the hooks and eyes on her bra. As I fumbled blindly with the cursed contraption, she whispered in my ear:

'You know, you should go and see that hypnotist… they're really close by.'

'What?'

'I said, you should go and see that hypnotist.'

'Yes, yes… Perhaps he can get this damned thing open!'

She slipped her hands behind her back and removed the stubborn undergarment in half a second. My inability to remove women's bras has always been a matter of intense annoyance to me, but I suppose I'm not the only man thus afflicted.

I closed my eyes and nuzzled my wife's breasts gently, tenderly, with my cheek. She went on:

'You should go… Are you listening?' I looked up at her, resting my chin between her breasts.

'What are you talking about?'

'About the hypnotist!' Her tone was sharp.

'Who cares about the hypnotist?' I murmured, burying my face in her breasts once more.

She pulled herself up on the bed.

'I do. I care!' She was shouting now. I stared at her, dumbfounded.

'Seriously?' I said. 'Here we are, together, relaxing, and all you can talk about is that nonsense of Pascal's.'

'It's not nonsense,' she retorted. 'He's given up smoking. He didn't light a single cigarette all evening.'

'He'll have a relapse.'

'He won't,' she said firmly.

'What's this all about?'

'It's about the fact that I've had... enough! There. I've had enough! Enough of the stink of stale tobacco everywhere, enough of your vile smoke, enough of finding ash all over the furniture, enough of emptying your ashtrays, enough of smelling smoke all over my clothes. Look! Just look at this bedroom, it's like making love in a giant ashtray. Your hair smells of cigarettes, your fingers are yellow, even your tongue tastes of tobacco.'

'My tongue? Well obviously, I've just smoked a cigarette...'

'Well I can't stand it a moment longer.'

Our marital tiff led me to a bright, calm, white-painted space. Marco di Caro's waiting room. Marco di Caro, the hypnotist. On the small glass coffee table, I took a photocopied sheet of paper from a pile clearly intended for his patients. I read all the evils that Monsieur di Caro claimed to cure.

My gaze wandered over the page: 'overcoming your fears, making a mental audit, finding the keys to your inner self...' The heading 'Compulsive urges' introduced an extended list:

'Compulsive drinking.

Compulsive drug use.

Compulsive nail-biting.

Compulsive snacking.

Compulsive washing (excessive washing).

Compulsive sleeping (all the time).

Compulsive scratching.

Compulsive smoking.

[…]'

There it was. I was the victim of a compulsive urge. What a charlatan, I thought. He opened the door. A huge, cheery-looking man with long hair and a grizzled beard. An imposing figure: these were the words that sprang to mind at this first sighting. He greeted me and showed me into his office.

I gave him my personal details – family name, first name, age, state of health – and he asked what had prompted my visit. I told him about the conversation with my friend Pascal, and my desire to quit smoking.

'You don't seem very convinced.'

'No. And to tell you the truth, I'm doing this for my wife. She's the one who forced me to come.'

'Forced you?' he asks, smiling.

'Yes… And I can tell you right now, this won't work with me. I've tried so many times, with no success, and I have no faith in hypnosis.'

'Come this way,' he says after a short silence.

I lie down on a big leather couch. He asks me to breathe deeply, to clear my mind, to picture a fine, white sandy beach, to feel the caress of the breeze, the soft sigh of the retreating waves, the sun on my skin, the softness of the sand, the soft grains of sand, grains of sand, grains of sand, grains of sand, grains of sand…

'Open your eyes.' I see the room all around me. How long had I been away from here? An hour? Ten minutes, two minutes, ten years?

★

Now I'm walking down the street.

'Try not to smoke in the next few hours.' His voice was making its way around my head like a small cloud of cotton wool. I felt like cotton wool, too. Overly rested, and yet perfectly wide awake.

I took a seat on a brasserie terrace and ordered a coffee. I sipped my sugary espresso and noticed that, strangely, I felt no urge to light a cigarette.

Compulsive snacking.

Compulsive itching.

Compulsive smoking…

The list of compulsive urges came back to me, like a children's nursery rhyme. Still sceptical, I decided that my non-desire to light up stemmed from my still-sleepy state. It was not possible. No way had it worked.

After dinner we watched a film: *The Swimming Pool*, with Alain Delon, Maurice Ronet and Romy Schneider. I barely noticed when one of the characters lit a cigarette. Everyone smokes in films from the sixties and seventies. Usually, they spark a mimetic impulse in me, the smoker-spectator. As the film came to an end, to the music by Saint-Preux, my wife nestled close and smiled.

'It's worked,' she whispered in my ear. I glanced at my ashtray. It was empty, clean, shining. Empty.

'Come, I want to make love right now.' My wife led me to the bedroom. It smelled different – the fragrance of fresh flowers pervaded the whole apartment. A scented candle, no doubt. She must have emptied all the ashtrays, opened all the windows for hours, chased away the smell that's been mine for so long.

Plainly, the fact that I hadn't smoked for half a day had stirred my wife to previously unattained heights of erotic excitement. I was perplexed, and made love to her, wondering what this would be like after two weeks without cigarettes.

The spell broke the next day. I was rocking in my office chair, and the movement led my eye to my desk drawer. Inside was my packet of Dunhills, almost full. My little blonde sweethearts were nestled up close, all together. It's over, I thought. Hypnosis has its uses, but it doesn't last. It wasn't a complete scam – I had held out for almost twenty-four hours, yes, a funny old thing, hypnosis, I told myself, as I removed a cigarette from the pack, a funny old thing indeed. It had worked, in a way. A supernatural phenomenon had occurred. I lit my cigarette, yes indeed, there were unexplored regions of the mind, I could see that…

Something interrupted my thoughts, something appalling, horrifying. And that something was NOTHING. The blue smoke had made its way, as usual, from my lips to my nostrils via my lungs. I froze in my chair, overcome with an uncontrollable feeling of panic. As if in slow motion, observing my every move, I repeated the operation.

NOTHING. I felt nothing at all.

The bitter, blonde taste of that first cigarette of the day, the intoxicating frisson in your brain when you take that first drag. That feeling of downing a strong, sweet gulp of alcohol along with the smoke, the sheer pleasure… yes, the pleasure. It had gone. Disappeared, extinguished. I sucked in my strong, blonde smoke, seeking the pleasure. It must be there, hiding somewhere, it would show itself, reappear.

It did not reappear. My cigarette tasted of nothing but a slightly dusty breath of warm air. I was broken. I stubbed the butt into my spotless ashtray and sat motionless for several minutes. If anyone had entered my office at that moment and seen my livid, pale face and staring eyes, they would surely have asked:

'What's the matter, have you lost someone close?'

And I would have replied:

'Yes. I've lost… my cigarettes.'

To me, the loss of my pleasure in smoking felt as if a whole section of my personality had come crashing down, never to be rebuilt. Worse, it felt as if I'd had a leg amputated, or an arm, that could never be grafted back into place. I'd been had. Robbed. I had never wanted to give up smoking. The hypnosis was only ever meant to quell my wife's anger.

Each individual's personality is a dense, complex jungle. Every one of the plants and species that comprise it plays an essential role, maintaining its balance. From the tallest tree to the tiniest mosquito. Remove even one link from the chain, and the whole ecosystem collapses. The extinction of one plant leads to the downfall of another species, which was food for another, and when that goes extinct, it takes with it the tree in which it lived, which affects the behaviour of a species of bird, and thence the lifecycle of a mammal.

Human beings are the same: childhood, adolescence, the pain of a failed love affair, your work, wife, money, apartment; all of these are aspects of our inner forest. If your wife leaves, or you're transferred to a new position at work, or you meet an old flame, or move to a new home, or lose someone, or some money, or find impossible to carry on playing a sport you loved, or if you lose your feelings of desire, or pleasure, it can tip a person over the edge, change them for ever – sometimes even destroy them. When that happens, people try desperately to get back to where they were before. They chase after the other, the person they once were, and the quest can take them to deep, sombre places. Their inner shadows lead them down the darkest passages of the soul, to depression, illness, suicide, murder or madness.

The police came to see me as part of their routine enquiries. They had found my name in Di Caro's diary. I told them how I had wanted to give up smoking. The inspector asked me if it had worked, because he'd been wanting to quit for years. When I told him the hypnosis session had worked perfectly, he shook his head miserably.

'If only I'd met that guy...' His last words as he shook my hand and walked out of my life for ever.

That was one year ago.

Since that day, I've decided to smoke just one cigarette a year, on the twelfth of March, at 4 p.m. precisely. The date and time at which Marco di Caro's head hit the chiselled cornice of his marble chimneypiece after a violent struggle that caused him to lose his balance. I light just one cigarette, at that exact moment each year. It has no taste. I do it for one reason only: to remind me of what I am. A murderer.

'It's the twelfth of March, four p.m. Aren't you going to light a cigarette, doctor?'

I stare at her. Nathalia has spoken these words without turning around. I open my desk drawer. The packet and the sky-blue Bic lighter are waiting inside. I take out a long, white cigarette, put the filter to my lips and snap the blue lighter.

I hear the tobacco's faint crackle as it catches alight. The first drag, taking the smoke down into my lungs, is followed by a long exhalation that sets my head spinning. The action delivers a sense of release so strong that I must close my eyes. And now I see it all. I see why I needed to know, from the outset, whether Nathalia's stories were true or false. Because I know she has aimed them at me all along.

The north wing, at the back of her courtyard. A place to which I've returned a thousand times and more in my mind's eye. Sometimes, I feel as if I've never left. I had no idea how true that was, until now.

'You lot make me laugh... shrinks, lawyers. You think you've got all the answers.'

'Go on.'

'There's nothing to "go on" about, doctor. There's nothing so pure and simple as murder, is all.'

'You think acting on an impulse to kill is a simple matter?'

'Very simple, believe me.'

A few years ago, this patient was referred to me by the crime squad, for three sessions of analysis as part of an investigation, to 'get an accurate picture of the individual's troubled personality'.

Patient P.S. had murdered his wife, his mistress and his boss, all on the same afternoon, and had allowed himself to be caught and arrested by the police, showing no resistance. I was mandated to trace the origins of his impulse, to find the dark recess where his demons lurked and to deduce their connection to profound childhood trauma or emotional upheaval as yet unidentified.

But there were no dark recesses. No demons.

'What is it you're after?' he asked me in a calm, matter-of-fact tone, while three armed officers sat outside in my waiting room. 'You won't find anything,' he added. 'I killed my boss because he'd been giving me shit for fourteen years, and the wife for the same reason, and my mistress. I got rid of them because they were making my life a misery.'

And for the first time, I found nothing to pick up on, no further questions to ask. I sat and listened, and his actions did indeed appear simple in the extreme. Hideously simple. He had acted not on some dark impulse, but on a straightforward decision, like any other. To take a train, ask for a woman's hand in marriage, resign from a job, kill someone.

'You think killing is a complicated business? Not at all, it's dead simple. Bodies are fragile things; a carefully directed hammer blow to the temple, a pillow over the face, a well-aimed point twenty-two rifle...'

'Your weapon.'

'Yes. Simplest way. Have you honestly never wished anyone dead, doctor?'

How to answer such a question? Yes, of course, like everyone – in theory. I wanted the student medic dead, who'd dated a stunning Italian girl I had my eye on, in our third year. Well... dead? I don't know if I would have been capable of tipping cyanide into his coffee, but, thinking about it, perhaps I would have done just that, in the heat of the moment. And then there was Framantonni, who took over as Chair of the Psychoanalytic Circle following Malevinsky's death, when the post should have gone to me. I had considered him a friend, and he had plotted behind my back, for months, while I suspected nothing. Darouelle, too, in our third year at medical school. A professor who was determined to bring me down, and succeeded, forcing me to take the year again after a vicious viva examination. He died that summer in a plane crash in southern Corsica, and when I heard the news in September, it felt like natural justice. Still, that day, the distance between thought and deed seemed vast.

'Do you see this as an impulsive act, or something pre-meditated?'

'Call it whatever you like, the time comes when you have to get it out of your system.'

'There was premeditation, in your case.'

'Yes. I'm an intelligent man, I had a few hours to think it over, and I made my choice.'

'You were motivated by anger?'

'Yes.'

'Had you ever felt yourself capable of such violence?'

'No.'

'Tell me about your parents, your family background.'

'Simple folk. Farmers from the Cantal, the sticks. Nothing much to say about them, or their friends. My childhood and teenage years were very happy. My sister too. She's still there, she runs a bar in Massiac.'

After a moment's silence, I told him that I could not state that he had acted as a result of diminished responsibility, or psychological troubles of any kind. This would affect his defence in court. His actions were inexcusable.

He got up from the couch, smiling broadly.

'Why are you smiling?'

'You must be disappointed. I'm not some twisted psycho-whatnot. Sorry, doctor.'

'That's precisely what terrifies me.'

'What?'

'Your normality.'

He said nothing, but when the three officers entered the room and applied their pointless handcuffs, P.S. turned to me with these words:

'Anyone can kill. It's as simple as lighting a cigarette.'

He jerked his chin at the police officers and showed his restrained hands. One of them searched in P.S.'s jacket, took out a pack of cigarettes and placed one between his lips. Then they patted their own pockets, in search of a lighter.

'I'm not allowed a lighter,' said P.S., grinning.

One of the officers looked at me.

'Do you have a light, professor?'

Who knows where my spurious professorship had come from, but I lit P.S.'s cigarette.

'Keep it,' I said, passing the lighter to one of the cops.

P.S. nodded in gratitude, and the four of them left my office. P.S. was a butcher by trade. His boss ran a well-known chain of shops – home-grown quality, reared in France. His wife was a sales assistant in the shop, and his mistress was married to the owner of the delicatessen and caterer's opposite.

He got thirty years. Anyone can kill. Yes, anyone, not least me. For the most senseless of motives. I had to get it out of my system. The butcher was right. Terrifyingly right. Anyone might kill, one day. They might even get away with it.

'The last photograph you took... Did you bring it with you?'

There are three, in fact.

Laid out on my desk, they resemble a triptych by Francis Bacon. Nathalia had chosen that afternoon to experiment with exposure times when photographing movement. She had no model but had positioned herself at the window with the aim of shooting the sunlight as it moved across the façade on the north side of her courtyard. In the darkroom, when the pictures were developed, she would see whether the light and movement had been captured to artistic effect. In place of a digital camera, she had chosen to use film, with a Rolleiflex and a very short focal length. Through the window on the fifth floor, she saw Di Caro asleep on a sofa. He would doze after his hypnosis sessions, it seemed, for about half an hour. He had been lying there for ten minutes, and Nathalia was watching him. He turned over on the sofa. Fearing he might see her and think she was spying on him, she took a step back from her window, hiding in the half-light of her apartment. It was then that I appeared.

It was then that she heard the first, faint rings on the bell. It was then that she saw my fist fly, saw us chase through the apartment, and the violent struggle that caused him to lose his balance – as she would later describe in her story.

No one heard the fight because there was no one on the fourth floor. Marc Lacour, the trader on the third floor, would have been sitting in front of his screens at La Défense, and below him, Vincent Véga, the lyricist, was thinking about a new song, with headphones over his ears and Belphégor the cat fast asleep on top of a pile of papers. On the first floor, Alban was listening to France Inter radio, bent over his drawing board. Alice Larjac, the life coach on the ground floor, was deep in a telephone consultation with one of her followers.

There was no one to hear, and only one pair of eyes to see. She took three photographs, with no time to adjust the settings on her camera.

Triptych of a Murder, by Nathalia Guitry and Doctor Faber:

Left: The dark mass of my back fills one half of the picture, dissecting it diagonally. Di Caro is looking up at me, his mouth is red, and the picture has captured his movement, swathing him in unfocused flesh pink and freezing the thrash and gleam of his eyes in white zigzags across the photograph.

Centre: Abstract motion. Di Caro's bloodied maw seems to holler across the whole of the picture, though he is already dead. Here, the long exposure has caught his mouth, to horrifying effect. He has multiple jaws and ten sets of teeth.

Right: A profile, clearly recognisable as mine, fleeing towards the left edge of the frame, with a great, black, spectral shadow in my wake.

It's me. That's my black jacket smudged across the picture, in striking contrast to my ghostly white profile, which is perfectly sharp and clear, as if incised with a scalpel. Everything around me is a blur of movement, frozen in time.

I was mad with rage at the hypnotist who had deprived me of the joy of cigarettes. I had gone to his apartment in a state of agitation, the like of which I had never experienced before.

Anger in its purest form. There was no one else there that day. If he'd been with a patient, or if his waiting room had been full, I would have been saved. Perhaps he hadn't taken any appointments that afternoon. I'll never know.

What I do know is that I rang the doorbell several times.

I can hear the sound of the bell now, long and tinkling. It grated on my nerves, heightening my tense, nervous state. When he opened the door, at last, I almost pushed it into him, and told him in a threatening tone to restore what he had taken from me. He stared at me smiling, then burst out laughing.

I think he found the situation highly amusing: the client, a smoker, listed under 'Compulsive urges', coming back to ask for his compulsive urge to be reinstated. Faber, the renowned psychoanalyst, a disciple of Malevinsky, at the mercy of a charlatan hypnotist. I saw his yellowed teeth, and the tea-stained look of his beard, both typical of a heavy smoker – details I had failed to notice the first time. And I thought to myself: you crook, you're a smoker, and you turn others against it in disgust. Traitor. He was still laughing when I threw my balled fist at the traitor's mouth. He fell backwards and then, as I stood staring at him, stupefied by what I had just done, he lifted his head to look at me, his mouth filled with blood.

He took me firmly by the arm and attempted to throw me out, but I ducked through to his consulting room, and he chased after me shouting:

'But it's all over, it's finished!'

Yes. Soon, it would all be over.

I remember putting my hands out in front of me, warding him off. I told him:

'I'm…. I'm sorry I hit you, but I'll pay… I'll pay you whatever you ask to lift this spell… Put me to sleep and give me back—'

Before I could get the words out, he had seized the collar of my black jacket, which tore in his grasp. I resisted. I fought to get free, and his bloodied mouth spoke the word 'insane' several times over. Then I threw his whole body backwards under his own weight, and he lost his balance. His head hit the jutting edge of the black marble chimneypiece and he crumpled to the floor. He was sitting motionless now, with his back to the fireplace, legs spreadeagled, eyes and mouth wide open. I couldn't hear his breathing. I knelt beside him and took his pulse. He was dead.

After that, I remember a door slamming, the stone steps on the staircase that seemed never-ending, and I felt I was running down to Hell itself. Me, a medical man, a man of reason… I had just killed another human being.

In the days that followed, the 'News in Brief' column of the daily paper *Le Parisien* reported the story, in characteristically succinct style:

Paris, 17th arrondissement: a professional hypnotist was found dead in his apartment by his cleaner. The time of death was put at two days prior, apparently after an altercation with a third party. The police investigation is focused on the man's patient list, and his family. His ex-wife and sister, with whom he was in dispute over an inheritance, were interviewed yesterday. The victim had no children, and no known partner.

Nathalia is sitting up on the couch, and I am stubbing out my cigarette.

'How did you find me?'

'I see you every day.'

'I don't understand.'

'Open your curtains, just as you do every evening at seven p.m., after your last consultation.'

I stare at her, then stand up and open the curtains wide. Sunlight floods into the room.

'You only went twice to the north wing, but it's been there all along, hasn't it?'

I look out at the blond stone building, the one I see every day from my windows, so close by. That was one of the factors that had decided me: I would never have crossed the city to consult a hypnotist, but I was prepared to cross the street. Nathalia had observed and inferred almost everything, her story was entirely true, apart from the renewed erotic charge between me and my wife. But I'll grant her that small inaccuracy.

'What you see is the street side of my building. The two open windows – that's me. When you ran out into the courtyard, all I had to do was cross to the other side of my apartment to see where you were going. You crossed the street, into this building. The next day, when you opened your curtains, I recognised your silhouette. That told me which floor you were on. The brass plate in the entrance gave me your name, and your profession.

I sit down beside the couch.

'All the rest, the other floors, was that all made up?'

'Yes and no. A bit of both. Alice Larjac really does live there, and her real name is really Marie-Edwige de La Tourrière. How did she get into life coaching online? I have no idea, and she never told me. She introduced Aïcha to me once, as her best friend, in a café. How did they meet? Again, I have no idea. I have no idea what Aïcha does, either. I made up the bit about her job as personal assistant to a very important boss. Perhaps that really is what she does. Or perhaps not at all. Alban is a real person, as you know. He has been on a diet, perhaps just for his own well-being, or to please a woman. But which woman? I have no idea. I met him in the hallway of the building, and I congratulated him on a drawing he did on Instagram during lockdown. He offered to give me the original. I went to his place, and his partner was there. She does the make-up for a TV show he appeared on, but I don't know if that's where they met. As for Marc Lacour, I have no idea if he met his partner at the Lady's Tower, nor if it really was the screensaver on his laptop, nor if he had a near-death experience. He did commission me to take that photograph, and he told me then that he'd been a trader, and that he wanted to make a radical life change. One day, I received the card for the Scottish guesthouse in the post, with a note inviting me to come and see them if ever I'm passing through. The tower features on their web page, on a list of the local sights. Vincent Véga lives with a black cat called Belphégor, and he does call her Madame. He's the father of a boy who suffers from asthma, but the cat is not the reason he left his wife: they divorced, is all. We met just after he'd moved in: the cat got out and he was looking for it in the courtyard. Belphégor had climbed the tree, I could see her from my window.'

'So you really took the photograph in the magazine?'

'Yes.'

'N.G.?'

'For Nathalia Guitry. And I'm no relation to Sacha Guitry. Shall I carry on up through the floors?'

'Please.'

'I couldn't say anything about the fourth floor,' she continued, 'because there's no one there, but there are no seals on the doors, and no dead old lady with a complicated will, or lack of one. People say the apartment belongs to the mayor of the seventeenth arrondissement, part of his property portfolio, but he doesn't want anyone to know, and there's no name beside the buzzer on the ground floor. Mademoiselle Hitahido has the apartment on the fifth floor. She's a Japanese lady who's had a lot of renovations done, but I've only seen her for two weeks around Fashion Week, and then not at all. The building manager says she's the daughter of a wealthy

Japanese industrialist, and the apartment is her Paris pied-à-terre, to which she hardly ever comes. I don't know any more than that. The only other thing that's true, and which I know for sure, is what happened up there on that same fifth floor, on the twelfth of March, at four o'clock in the afternoon, one year ago.'

Were it not for our ghastly shared secret, I should feel a great and sincere sense of satisfaction: Nathalia is by far the most successful case of my career.

The patient–shrink relationship is an unnatural duo: two people who do not know one another meet in a room, yet what is said there comes from the most intimate, deepest chambers of the soul. It's an exercise of extreme precision, and complete trust. At conferences, I often compare it to a duo on the flying trapeze: every figure is executed with precision and trust, and it is impossible to tell which of the two is the stronger. We watch an aerial ballet whose beauty resides in its apparent simplicity.

The work of analysis possesses that same quiet beauty, that same, deceptively simple aesthetic: the patient reclining on the couch, always in the same position, and me sitting nearby, always in the same place, amid the same surroundings. Our exchanges are like acrobatic figures. Sometimes I guide the patient, and sometimes the patient leads me to the questions they want to hear.

Sometimes the patient will have spent years longing to hear those questions. Analysis is a slow preparation for the moment when they are heard. A rehearsal. A practice studio for a performance that will never take place within the consulting room. A performance I will never see: that of the patient in harmony with their own self, in the world outside my walls.

In real life. When they are equipped at last to navigate the obstacles they encounter. Because the obstacles are not eliminated: what went before is never erased, never obliterated. Everything remains. Like gravity, which can never be divorced from the performance on the high trapeze. On the contrary, it is integral to the artists' every move. Without it, there would be no performance, no skill, no beauty. And no danger.

'We need the undertow of gravity in our lives,' I tell my conference attendees. 'Without it, we would be weightless, superficial creatures with no bearings, empty as the air. Like fairground helium balloons that float off into the sky, going nowhere, drawn upwards on a rising air current to get stuck in the branches of a tree along with the supermarket plastic bags.'

The weightier our baggage, the wealthier we are, the more twisted our secrets, the more we know we are alive. We suffer burning doubts and remorse, we suffer our memories. We are scorched by our past actions. But we get burned because we are in possession of a body. The very worst moments in life are those when we feel most alive. The work of analysis focuses on that 'other body', in Malevinsky's words. The high-flying acrobatics of the soul, the exercise of the mind, so precise, so complex, that it can take us outside our own selves. Into the void, the silence, the struggle to resist the lure of gravity, just like the artists on the flying trapeze.

★

I look at Nathalia. She is sitting upright on the couch. I know what it means when the patient holds that position for a few too many seconds, and the seconds become a minute. The work is finished. The analysis is at an end.

'Let's have another cigarette,' she says.

I turn to where the red packet lies, but before I help myself, I hold it out to her. She takes one, lights it, then holds the lighter flame out to mine.

We smoke in silence. We have shattered the traditional therapeutic ceiling. The shrink and the patient have each broken open their secret – the same secret, as it happens. Together they have laid down their shared burden. To my knowledge, this has never happened before. It's as if we have entered an antechamber of sorts, leading to a state of untrammelled meta-conscience. We stand at the very top of the building, above the fifth floor. We have risen through the ceiling, the attic, the roof timbers, the zinc. We are floating weightless in a bright blue sky.

'Why are you smiling?' she asks me.

'I was thinking about a phrase of Jung's... I never really understood it: "Our destiny is the external manifestation of our internal subconscious conflicts."'

Nathalia takes a drag on her cigarette.

'I see what it means. I am your destiny.'

I gaze at her and I'm happy to see the tiniest hint of a smile playing at the corners of her lips. It proves to me that she has found freedom, too. She, too, is floating above the rooftop, in the blue sky.

'Now,' she says, 'I must do something symbolic. Something I've been waiting to do for a whole year.'

'What's that?'

'I won't call the police, if that's what you're thinking – if it was that, I would have done it a long time ago, and in any case it won't bring Di Caro back. No, what I want is for you to give back what you stole from me.'

'What did I steal?'

'My talent. I told you, that's why I came.'

She bends over her black canvas bag and takes out a brown paper envelope like the others containing her stories. She hands it to me. It isn't sealed, and there are no sheets of paper inside. I shake it upside down, and three photographic negatives slide out into the palm of my hand. Three tiny squares that contain the most terrifying moments of my life.

'Only you and I know what happened on the twelfth of March,' she says. 'For a year now, a part of you has stayed stuck inside my apartment. It's poisoning me, and I'm delivering myself from its clutches by returning it to you. There, they're yours.'

Nathalia is wrong when she states that we are the only two people who know what happened on the twelfth of March. Since this morning, my wife is in on the secret. The character in the final story is sure to remind her very much of me. She will remember the police coming to question me after Marco di Caro's violent death. But I'll see about that later. For the moment, Nathalia is still here. Not for much longer. She will be leaving soon. Already, she's stubbing out her cigarette in the ashtray and we are returning to Earth, to the pull of gravity.

Already, our sublime fusion is dissolving, which is perfectly normal. No creature can survive for long in the ecstasy of perfect knowledge. Such moments are rare, and the floors rise past us as we descend. We slip like feathers over the zinc rooftop, past the Persian blinds of the attic rooms on the sixth floor, past the windows of the fifth, where the now silent apartment awaits its rich Japanese occupant, past the windows of the fourth floor, whose empty rooms are counted in square metres for a speculative public official, past the third floor, its shutters long since closed, while far away on the Scottish coast, its former owner sips a whisky while he waits for Mary to come home. Behind the balcony on the second floor, there is no one in but Belphégor, snatching at a fly through the sheer curtains, while on the first floor we see Alban's drawing board, and his ink pots. And now, as we alight on the ground floor, we glimpse the huge blue lithograph by Jacques Monory, and Alice Larjac's camera, the one she uses to film herself. There. Our feet touch the cracks between the cobbles. Behind us stands a tall tree. No one has ever quite determined its species; some people in the building see a wild cherry, others an oak, though it has never produced an acorn.

'I knew you had "something of mine",' I say in a low voice.

I will never tell her about the curious feeling that came over me in my daughter's old room, on that morning when I thought it was summer, and Alain Bashung intoned the lines of his bizarre poem, like beads on a rosary. That feeling more powerful than love – the urgent desire for Nathalia to be my daughter.

Now she's about to leave. In a few moments the door of my

office, and then my apartment, will close behind her, and I will never see her again.

At the thought of it, something tightens inside me – something emotional and physical all at once. It began a few seconds ago, and I know all too well what it is. I am a doctor.

'I've got something for you, too,' I tell her.

She came home from the paper to find me waiting for her, sitting behind my desk. She pushed the door of my consulting room and walked towards me. She said nothing, then turned to look at the fire, which is never normally lit but was now devouring Nathalia's negatives and prints, and the stories from each floor of her building. She stood facing me, and we stared at one another in silence. Then she lowered her eyes to my desk. To the place where my collection of nine wrought-iron keys should have been laid out in meticulous order, each one with its sliding heart-shaped ring. My wife nodded silently, then looked back to the fireplace. She had a question, I could tell. She said:

'The stories were all made up, weren't they?'

And with not a shred of remorse – for if I must pay one day, it will not be in this life but in another, improbable place, before the great analyst himself, the one no one pays in cash, and whose work lasts for all eternity – yes, with not a shred of remorse, I answer:

'Of course. They were all fiction.'

That was when the pain tightened its grip once and for all. First in the left arm, then rising rapidly to my chest, turning my blood to poison. I asked my wife to give me a moment alone. The pain was worse, more oppressive still with each pulse of the aorta, spreading across my rib cage like an ink stain on blotting paper. My face turned grey and my hands felt like ice.

As my blood turned to ink and my heart rate wavered, I decided it was better this way. I thought of Catherine, my distant daughter for whom I had not been an ideal father, and who would doubtless now find qualities in me which I never possessed. The image of the blue-and-yellow parrot came to me, and I smiled as I remembered the bird's supposed longevity. It would certainly outlive me now.

With a superhuman effort, I got to my feet and did what I had never done before: I lay down on the couch.

In my final seconds, I thought of Nathalia, and my passe-partout keys, which she had taken with her. She would open other doors now. As for me, the locks were closing all around. My wife's strange comment – 'perhaps she isn't real' – taunted me no longer. On the contrary, in the blur of my last moments, I confused her words with Jung's statement on destiny. Finally, I saw Nathalia's face. This time, I had no difficulty recalling her appearance – she came to me with supernatural clarity, until at last it occurred to me that she was my appointment with death. I had never pictured Death as one so lovely, so sweet, with such blue eyes. Her face came close to my own; I held her to me and ran my hands through her shining hair, my cheek against her neck, and when I lost consciousness, I felt a joy that is not of this world.

One week later, I opened my eyes beneath a plain white ceiling. I gathered that this was not Paradise, nor Hell, nor purgatory, but a hospital ward – probably the ICU. I had no sense of time, and it was impossible for me to say whether I had been here for a few hours, or days, even weeks. My last memory was of lying stretched out on the couch. Just a few minutes ago. But no. A week had gone by. For my heart bypass operation, I had been put into an artificial coma, and I had woken up in the post-operative unit. François, my cardiologist friend, was the first face I saw bending over me. He touched my hand.

'It's all right, you've come through,' he told me. And I nodded slowly.

Unlike Nathalia's character – the trader who moved to Scotland – I had not floated outside my own body, nor passed through a tunnel of light. There was no NDE to report. I was discharged from the ICU after that, and now here I am, in this room.

My wife had come back into my office and found me lying unconscious on the couch. She had called for an ambulance immediately. The secretarial service that books my appointments had cleared my diary. I would be out in ten days' time. One week, plus ten days. I wondered what would become of them all. Robotti had sent flowers to the apartment, and my young anorexic had done the same, a bouquet of orange flowers – roses and gerberas – to which she had added a bunch of carrots. Robotti had written a note: 'Come back soon.' My anorexic hadn't written anything, but I was greatly touched by her gesture.

My wife and I have said nothing more about Nathalia's last story. All she asked was:

'Why did you give her the keys?'

I smiled. 'To give someone their keys' has a psychoanalytic ring to it.

'The collection was complete,' I mumbled, before pretending to fall asleep.

I believe I truly gave my wife a fright. The heart attack may even have brought us closer, though that remains to be seen. My daughter visited yesterday, and she seemed genuinely sorry to see me like this. She spoke some kind words, and then she said nothing at all. She walked over to the window and looked out at the apartment buildings opposite. In silence. Then she said she had to go.

I sit up in my hospital bed and reach for my phone, on the bedside table next to a glass of water. My fingerprint calls up a bank of icons. I hesitate, then press Contacts, and the letter N.

WHAT ARE YOU UP TO?

I put the phone down on the bed. Barely a minute goes by before a ringing sound signals an answering text message.

I'M AT HOME. JUST BACK FROM A SHOOT. I'M GOING TO POUR A GLASS OF WHITE WINE AND DRINK IT ON THE BALCONY. THE SUN IS SHINING. WHAT ABOUT YOU?

I'M IN HOSPITAL. I HAD A HEART ATTACK AFTER YOU LEFT. WHERE ARE YOU?

I gave her the name of the hospital, and my room number. She told me she was on her way. One hour later, I hear a knock at the door. I call for her to come in, and in she comes. Her blue eyes gaze at me, then she sits in the chair provided for visitors, right next to the bed. Gently, she places her hand on mine, then removes it, just as gently.

'So you're taking photographs again?'
She smiles.
'Yes, and what about you? Are you OK?'
'Better,' I tell her. 'Thank you for coming.'
She smiles, and I smile too. I realise I haven't smiled once since I've been here.
'The set-up is reversed,' I tell her.
She stares at me quizzically.
'I'm lying down, and you're sitting next to me.'
'Yes,' she says, with the same affirmative tone she used in our sessions.
'How's my collection of keys?'
'Great. I've set them out on a coffee table. How are my negatives?'

'I burned them.'

She blinks her approval then gets up and stands in front of the window, gazing out at the city's apartment buildings. In the exact spot where Catherine stood a few days before.

'In a way, it was me who got psychoanalysed by you, Nathalia,' I tell her.

I see her nod, but she does not turn around.

'And me?' she says, still gazing out at the city.

'What do you mean?'

'Is my analysis finished?'

A silence falls between us, which I choose to break by asking her:

'What are you thinking about?'

'About my balcony. Just now, I was drinking a glass of white wine in the sun. I was looking at the west wing.'

'You can see the west side of the building?'

'Yes.'

'What were you looking at?'

'The third floor. There was a lunch at Hélène Le Garrec's. She's an excellent cook. She's transformed her apartment into a pop-up restaurant. She sets out anything up to twenty covers, and people come on Thursday lunchtime and Saturday evenings. You have to be invited to join, you book online and there's a password to give over the intercom.'

'What was today's dish?'

'Quails in apple brandy with sauté potatoes, and girolles and morel mushrooms.'

'Nathalia?'

'Doctor Faber?'

'How many floors are there on the west side?'

'Five.'

She turns and smiles, fixing me with her clear gaze. She's breathing a little faster, I can tell. I know, now, that we will go back inside the building. The carriage door did not close on her. No. The story-telling will resume, a sign that the therapy is not over; that there are other secrets, and Nathalia will reveal them, rising up once again through the floors.

'We'll go straight to the third floor, for a change,' I say.

'Yes. When do you get out?'

'In ten days' time.'

'I'll come on the Thursday after that, then. Four o'clock, as usual?'

'Yes. Thursday. Four o'clock. I'll be expecting you, Nathalia.'

'I'll be there, doctor. Shall I bring my story over beforehand?'

'Perfect. Let's not change a thing. Not ever.'